STRAY

Nancy J. Hedin

A NineStar Press Publication

Published by NineStar Press
P.O. Box 91792,
Albuquerque, New Mexico, 87199 USA.
www.ninestarpress.com

Stray

Printed in the USA
First Edition
August, 2019

Print ISBN: 978-1-951057-21-3

Also available in eBook, ISBN: 978-1-951057-20-6

Warning: This book contains sexual content, which may only be suitable for mature readers, and homophobic violence and slurs.

Praise for Bend

Bend is a coming of age novel set in rural Minnesota. Seventeen-year-old twin daughters—one gay—one straight and Momma loves the straight one a little more, both girls are competing for the same scholarship to get out of town. There's a little mystery, a little romance, two dead bodies and a car chase, but it ends in Grace.

Bend (ISBN 978-1-62649-551-7) is available in trade paperback and eBook.

Bend was a finalist for the 2017 Foreword INDIES Book of the year in LGBT Adult and YA Fiction and won honorable mention in LGBT Adult Fiction. Bend was a finalist for the 2017 Golden Crown Literary Society Awards in the categories of General Fiction and Debut Novel and won Debut Novel.

In June of 2018 Barnes and Nobel named Bend one of twenty-five books to read for Pride Month. In June of 2019 Barnes and Nobel again named Bend a good read for Pride Month.

Rachel Wexelbaum in her September 21, 2017 Lambda review of Bend wrote,

"Coming out stories remain a popular genre among the LGBTQ community. We have strong memories about our individual experiences, complete with family and community conflict arising from our emerging queerness. Not only that, but the coming out experience of folks from conservative religious rural communities seems to transcend generational differences. These reasons, along with what I will share in this review, will make the new lesbian novel Bend a classic."

And she wrote, "Read Bend carefully, for it provides a formula for what a queer kid needs to build resilience and adapt to new experiences and environments."

Lambda Award Winning Author and Edgar Grand Master Award Winner, Ellen Hart said, "Bend is wonderfully rich. Hedin's voice is pitch perfect. You won't be disappointed."

All the literature I create is dedicated to my wife, Tracy, my daughters, Sophia and Emma, and in memory of my mom, dad, and brother, David.

Chapter One

IT WAS SUPPER time on a weeknight and there were two vehicles I didn't recognize and a hearse parked next to our farmhouse. It wasn't really a hearse, it was Pastor Grind's tan Toyota, but any visit from him meant bad news. God how I hoped Momma had started a book club or extorted people to attend a Tupperware party. More likely she was bringing me a parade of potential husbands. She wanted to straighten out her queer daughter, me. I didn't know if she was acting alone or if she'd again claim she had God on her side. Maybe she got Pastor Grind to agree to marry me to one of those men on the spot.

"Lorraine, Lorraine!" Momma came rumbling out of the house onto the open front porch, waving her arms. "Don't change out of your college clothes. We have guests for dinner."

It's not like I routinely changed clothes in the yard. I parked my truck in between Dad's beat-up pickup and Momma's dented station wagon. Momma had parked on half the pink flamingo pair of lawn ornaments Dad had installed the day before.

"We're having chicken. Ricky wants to learn to make my gravy." Momma wiped her hands on her denim apron.

Before I could ask her who Ricky was—*like I didn't already know he's some guy she found at college and deems him a good husband for me—the only requirement being a penis in his pants*—she put her hands on her wide hips like she had more to say. "That Charity girl is here too, but she's not staying." Momma swiveled around and marched to the house.

My girlfriend, Charity, was there. Finally, some good news. At least it meant she was driving her dad's car and he wasn't with her. There was no way that holier-than-god man would come to the queer's house and have his daughter with him.

Dad and my three-year-old nephew, Little Man, came out of the barn with the dogs, Sniff, Pants, and Satan. Dad was telling Little Man some damn animal story— something about what they can tell from smelling another dog's pee. Little Man and the dogs came running to me. "Raine, Raine, we've been throwing balls for the dogs."

Most days I took care of Little Man, but Tuesday was a school day for me at the junior college where I had enrolled in as many math and science classes as I could manage until I left for Grayson School of Veterinary Science in Duluth. Grayson wasn't a top ten veterinary school, but it was my first choice because I didn't have to have a bachelor's degree before entering their program. That was good for me since I had already delayed my college entrance by a couple of years because of the needs of my family.

Grayson accepted two years of college level science and math and allowed degree candidates to take summer classes for the entire four years of pre-veterinary science programs. It floated my boat, but what really got me excited was if I was short on the college level courses, which I was, they'd let me take skills and knowledge testing which would count toward coursework. All those things I'd learned from helping Twitch with his vet business could be parlayed for course credits. *Sweet.*

Little Man hugged my legs. When I looked at him and Momma and Dad, I had a hollow ache in my chest for who was missing. My twin sister, Becky, was dead. She left behind a dope of a husband and the sweetest little boy I could imagine existed in the world. My brother-in-law Kenny's truck was gone. He must have still been at work at the lumber yard.

I scooped up Little Man. He wore the matching blue and white T-shirt and pants I'd put him in early in the morning, but he was filthy from playing. As I kissed his doughy neck, I sniffed him to know what he'd done while I was away. I detected the scent of outdoors, dogs, dirt, and snickerdoodle cookies, an average day.

I dropped him off in the mudroom. He climbed the green plastic, frog-faced step stool so he could reach the mudroom sink to wash his hands, and I looked for Charity. Charity leaned against the kitchen counter. *Damn she looks good.* I forgot all about supper. My whole body hungered for her touch and the sweet things she always said to me. I wanted to wrap my arms around Charity and kiss her until my lips fell off.

No kissing for me. Momma came back in the kitchen looking like she owned and ran the place, which she did. Momma and Charity were as far apart from each other as possible in the room and despite the temperature outside being near eighty degrees, the air temperature between them was colder than a well-digger's lunch, as my dad would say.

"Hi." I touched Charity's shoulder. "I'm glad to see you. Why are you driving your dad's car? You about scared me to death."

She smiled and squeezed my hand quick, her eyes glued on Momma. "Dad needed my truck to help somebody move some boxes or something."

I smelled her shampoo and she'd just put on some lip gloss I wanted to methodically taste and remove.

Momma gave the queer girls only cursory attention. I almost snuck a kiss, but I realized half a man twitched and kicked on the kitchen floor. The other half of him was tucked in the cabinet under the sink. When the top of him emerged I about lost my mind.

Christ, she's at it again. This time the man was old enough to have possibly signed the Declaration of Independence, or at least the Constitution.

"Momma, I hope you haven't been trying to find a date for me again." Next, I addressed the fossil under the sink. "Ricky, I'm sorry you come all this way for nothing but a busted sink."

Just then Little Man came in the kitchen. Momma's face brightened as she whisked Little Man into her arms. He dried his wet hands on the front of Momma's good apron—the full-length one with chickens embroidered on it and pockets on both sides of the skirt. Next Momma pulled me into the utility room with her and Little Man. "Excuse us." She slid the accordion door closed.

Oh Christ, she's going to murder me. No. She wouldn't murder me in front of Little Man and so many witnesses in the house, but there was a fair chance she was going to lecture me and possibly brain me with one of her sacred books. She appreciated the Old Testament shock and awe. She didn't much go for the patient tolerance of God's later work or "the mushy parts," as she called them. However, she did like the way her slim New Testament fit in the oversized pockets of her denim apron, and she liked the way it fit nicely in her hand when she wanted to swat someone, usually me. But she didn't hit me. Instead, she reminded me of the way her mind worked and how she got everything done with speed and efficiency.

"That's not Ricky. It's Harold. Has it ever occurred to you, Lorraine, that we needed the sink replaced?"

That's Momma for you. She could probably kill more than two birds with one stone. She weaseled getting our sink fixed *and* paraded a bachelor for my appraisal. She was so efficient, I was surprised there were any birds left.

Momma continued, "Besides, you can't marry Harold. He's already engaged to a gal from the square-dancing club."

"Square dancing," Little Man said.

Little Man, at three years old, needed an interpreter. I caught most everything he said because I listened to him most days. He had acquired a new habit of repeating parts of whatever he'd heard somebody else say.

"Well, do-si-do and an allemande right if I'm not relieved."

"Smarty pants," Momma said. "Behave yourself. It wouldn't hurt you to try to make friends with our guests. Supper is almost ready."

"Great. I want to sit by Charity."

"She's not staying."

What? Hadn't we made any ground at all? Couldn't my girlfriend at least enjoy a meal at our house? It's not like we would make out at the dinner table.

Momma pushed me out of the utility room, put Little Man down with half a cookie, and helped Harold get up off the kitchen floor.

"Can't you stay for supper?" I asked Charity.

Charity glanced at Momma. Then she looked at her feet and bit her lip.

Those lips. I knew how pillowy soft and warm they were. The first time she ever kissed me it felt like I had known her mouth forever.

Charity turned her back on Momma and she half whispered and half gasped, "Lorraine, are you ever leaving for college? This is too small, too much."

"How can something be both too small and too much?" I tried to joke, but Charity wasn't having it.

"I don't know, but Bend is and you need to decide. I'm going home." Charity headed to the door.

I wanted to remind her I was moving as fast as circumstances would allow. I'd enrolled in as many science classes as the junior college offered while I worked with Twitch...and I minded Little Man. But I didn't speak up for myself.

"Are you still coming over tomorrow?" I whispered. "Little Man has some new plastic animals. I'm thinking of decorating the kitchen like an African safari." My scheme kept Little Man busy and allowed me to study animal physiology and anatomy at the same time.

"See you tomorrow." Charity called over her shoulder with very little enthusiasm.

I watched Charity through the window walking away. My heart raced. I almost ran after her, but then Momma grabbed me and harped at me to go sit in the dining room and talk to the guests. *Why is everybody so mad at me? Why is everyone pressuring me to move faster or be different?* Momma wanted me to not be queer and marry a man. Charity wanted me to leave Bend before I had Little Man settled. I took deep breaths and prepared to enter the dining room.

Chapter Two

MOMMA COULDN'T REALLY blame me for assuming she'd brought Harold home for me. Even though a year ago she'd said she would try to understand the continuum of sexuality in the animal kingdom, she leaned more toward spouting damnation for queers. She had once, during a weakened state, given me a note with "bonobos" written on it. Per our family tradition mostly instituted and observed by my dad, I was supposed to take it to the library and learn a lesson from researching the topic on the note. I learned that Bonobos are very sexual primates and they engage in homosexual sex too. Even though the gesture made it seem like Momma understood and accepted my sexuality, she didn't. Her religion wouldn't let her, or maybe she blamed religion for her own fear and hate. She made it abundantly clear she had continued to pray I'd straighten out.

Of course, my momma could not leave such important tasks to prayer and the whims of God. She trolled the dual campus of St. Wendell's new junior college and technical college looking for single men who would, in her mind, properly scratch my itch. Without warning or apology, she brought these strangers home for dinner. The men were an unlikely posse of testosterone, practical skills, and kind hearts. Momma exploited their practical skills to repair our house and vehicles.

This "guess who's coming to dinner" farce had gone on the entire first year of Momma's two-year nursing program and didn't seem to be letting up even though Momma had completed her core classes and started her clinicals in the community. I wondered which bachelor she had coming to dinner? It could have been Russ, a barrel-chested Norwegian with hands like fielder's mitts who was a second-year mechanic when Momma met him. Maybe Melvin, a thin wiry German who studied carpentry at the technical college, sat at our table. Once Momma got a hold of him, he came to our farm to meet me. He got nowhere in the courtship, but Momma got him to build a combination tree house and secret fort for Little Man and he helped Kenny and Dad finish the upstairs of the farmhouse, which added another bedroom and a bathroom.

After Charity left the yard, I noticed the asthmatic plumber who courted the square dancer had packed up and was heading out the door. I peeked into the dining room. Russ the mechanic sat at our table alongside a young woman I didn't know.

"If you want to see some of my best matchmaking, see how Kenny reacts to Russ' sister, Ramona," Momma whispered to me as she went by carrying a bowl of mashed potatoes in one hand and a bowl of chicken gravy in the other. "I think those two would be perfect for each other and she'd make a good momma for Little Man."

Crap.

As I scrutinized this woman Momma picked out for Kenny, my attention wandered to an awfully good looking young man. He sat next to Momma and flirted with her. I sat in the empty chair on the other side of Momma.

"I want you to teach me to cook like you, Mrs. T," he said.

Momma stopped serving the food and sat next to the young man. "Call me Peggy." Momma sited me in. "Lorraine, this is Ricky."

So that's Ricky. Dad had taught me to see the animal in people. When I looked at Ricky I saw a chipmunk. Cute, soft, delicate bones of a bird, and eyes a person could fall into just before he darted up a tree or over a log.

Momma grinned broadly and nodded toward the man like she was telepathically telling me something or willing me to fall in love with him on the spot.

"Hello, Lorraine," he said. "I hope you don't mind I love your mother?"

I glanced at Dad, the head of the table. He'd never been the head of anything in this family, except for the yard he filled up with bobbles, garden gnomes, and plastic animal tableaus. Even those things Momma removed or accidently ran over at will. Momma called the shots. Dad sat at the head of the table but might just as well have been in the barn or still at work at the lumber yard. He didn't say anything. He just watched.

I smiled at Ricky. "No, I don't mind. You can take Momma home with you if you like."

Momma put her hand on my sleeve and gripped my wrist like I'd said something wrong.

"What'd I say?" I looked at Momma, Dad, and back at Ricky.

"It's okay, Peggy," Ricky said to Momma. He turned to me. "Lorraine, your Momma worries because I'm homeless, but I'll be fine. Peggy, will you teach me to make gravy?"

"It's flour, drippings, and milk or water," I said as I scooped mashed potatoes on my plate. "It's not like you're cooking methamphetamines."

Momma grabbed my wrist again tight enough to stop the flow of blood to my hand. She tipped my plate of potatoes back in the bowl. Her gaze remained zeroed in on me as she grabbed her purse with her free hand. She positioned the purse so she could reach it—conceal and carry. At any moment Momma would pull out her register of reckoning, her notebook. The spiral-bound journal, volume twenty-six if the front cover was accurate, was Momma's way of keeping track of our family's transgressions and her list of things she wanted the rest of us to do.

"Oh no, Peggy. You needn't mark your book for me. There's no harm done." Ricky batted his unusually long beautiful lashes at Momma.

What a suck-up! How long had they known each other? They were already protecting each other's feelings? *Yuck.*

Momma let go of my wrist and petted Ricky. "I'm not listing more of Lorraine's sins, dear. I just want us to join together in grace before she puts her mitts on the food. Pass this to Joseph. The page is marked."

The dinner guests passed Momma's notebook hand to hand around the table until it reached Dad. The pencil dangled from a string tied to the notebook. Momma had two remaining sets of Biblical themed pencils she used to write in the notebook. I couldn't tell if the ten commandments or one of the eight Beatitudes dragged through the salad and rolls.

I covered my face with my hand and watched through my fingers as the notebook reached my dad. He stared at Momma. His wind and sun-beaten face reddening. He knew the drill. We both knew the drill. He'd been conscripted to read from her notebook before and it had never been pretty or the words of his own heart. He didn't challenge Momma on this any more than he challenged her on anything else. Dad managed the yard. Everything demanded, declared, and determined belonged to Momma.

"Once Kenny gets here, Joseph will lead us in a prayer of thanksgiving for this food and the young hearts around this table."

"I can't wait to eat more of your cooking, Peggy." Ricky purred.

My momma may have responded to flattery about her beauty, her intelligence, or her fortitude, but she became as pliable as taffy when someone gushed about her cooking. It wasn't that she didn't know she was good. She knew. But she needed to hear it from others . Dad and Kenny made a big deal about every meal, gushing, mmmming. Granted, my momma was the best cook in the world in my book too, but I didn't think it had to be stated every minute. Ricky's fawning nauseated me; worse yet, he asked for Momma's counsel.

Momma scurried back to the kitchen again and brought back two bowls of steaming vegetables.

"We'll cook together. That's our destiny." He looked at me. "Gravy is an art." He turned again to Momma. "I want to learn it all—beef, pork, chicken, when to use water or milk, how to thicken it. What are your tricks for making it an appetizing color?"

"Sounds like you already know a lot," Momma said, stroking his rich, dark hair.

"But there is so much, Peggy—the color, the consistency, the flavor. A good gravy can make a meal, don't you think?"

"How did you get to be so wise? Ricky, you're the daughter I never had. A daughter who wants to learn at my bosom." *Good grief.* Momma put her big hand to her bountiful chest. "Becky's gone, and Lorraine would live on canned soup and sandwiches if I didn't cook."

"My God, you two should get a room." I rolled my eyes and laughed.

"Lorraine," Dad said.

Oops. Dad warned me to watch my phraseology. He didn't fight Momma on much, but he would not abide anyone showing her disrespect.

"Ricky grew up in St. Wendel," Momma said. "He's half Mexican and half Swede. Can you imagine that?"

Of course, I had no trouble imagining it. It wasn't like his parents crossed species. I learned he'd been out of the house since age sixteen and studied cosmetology at the technical school. *Ding, ding, ding!* I didn't want him as a boyfriend, but I strongly doubted he wanted me or any other woman as a girlfriend. I suspected he was queer too. Before I could test my theory, Kenny came home from work and the farce worsened.

Kenny had worshipped, married, and impregnated my sister Becky, not necessarily in that order. Since Becky's death, Kenny and Little Man had been living with our family on the farm and Kenny had finished his GED and worked with Dad at the lumber yard.

I wanted Kenny to have someone. Hell, I'd have given him to anyone who'd be stupid enough to take him, but I didn't want to lose Little Man. I wanted Little Man close, so I could keep him safe. I had failed Becky and she died. Her death was mine to carry. I refused to lose anyone I loved again.

Kenny, the horndog, spotted Ramona immediately. *Christ, he's ogling her.* I wondered if he knew Momma had picked her out as his next wife. It was hard to watch. Granted, Ramona had many fine, noticeable features. She was a year younger than me—Kenny's age. Her soft brown curls fell in waves along her face and onto her shoulders, in contrast to my wild curls which looked like they'd been trapped for the better part of a century in a jack-in-the-box.

Ramona had a slim waist, long limbs, and tiny hands. She wore a khaki skirt with a coral knit shell and stylish sandals. She told me she studied child development at the technical school, but she lived at home with Russ and cared for their mother who had MS.

Great. She's good looking, knows about kids, and she's a candidate for sainthood. Of course, Kenny would fall in love with her. An alarm went off in my head and my heart raced. If Kenny fell in love with her, he would take Little Man away from our house. *Crap.* I started to hyperventilate. I needed space, air, and certainly lots of potatoes. I couldn't let them fall in love. I couldn't let them talk together. I couldn't chance losing Little Man.

"Kenny, remember this is the time of day I tell you three sweet things and three mischievous things Little Man did during the day. I had class today, so I missed some things, but I still know some doozies." I grabbed his arm once I could reach him. I don't think I had voluntarily touched him ever before in my life. The big dope. Couldn't he see by my face how much I needed him to keep Little Man with me?

"Maybe we should take our plates in the kitchen and I'll tell you all about it. I know you hate missing out on these things while you're at work and mourning the death of your recently deceased wife and my sister, Becky."

"Lorraine, are you all right? You're being weirder than usual." Kenny narrowed his eyes at me and pulled loose from my grasp.

"I'm not being weirder than usual. I just thought you would want to hear about your son's day." I reached for the potatoes again. Momma slapped my hand and placed the fried chicken in front of Ramona.

"I do want to hear about my son's day," Kenny said. "Just not right now."

That dumbass, ungrateful, testosterone-addled ape had brushed me off. Not only that, Kenny swaggered. Well, he swaggered as much as anybody could swagger in our dining room with leaves in the table and four adults and one pipsqueak seated there waiting for supper while my wide-hipped momma scuttled between the kitchen and dining room serving the meal. I'd offered to help serve, but she told me to go talk with Russ and Ricky.

"I'm Kenny Hollister," he said to Ramona. "I was married to Becky Tyler, but she died a while back."

"Died." Little Man said it without emotion or loss. He kicked the table leg rhythmically from his booster chair.

Ramona said her obligatory sorries and reached over and squeezed Little Man's hand.

I hated her, but I hated Kenny even more. How could Kenny be so casual in the way he mentioned Becky's death? Why didn't he tell Ramona what happened? Let him try to describe Becky's death. No big deal, my ass. Tell Ramona Becky killed herself during a psychotic episode? Why didn't he say she got mentally ill, stopped her medications, stabbed herself, doused herself with gasoline, and dropped into a fire she had at first prepared for Little Man. He didn't say none of the hard stuff I saw and dreamed about every night of my life since. He didn't say it; he just acted like the rest of us weren't there. We were very much alive and had been taking care of his son full time.

"Well, Kenny, you better wash up." *Christ, I sound like* Momma.

Kenny's eyes narrowed when he looked at me and he turned his head like a confused cocker spaniel. He took the empty chair next to Ramona.

"I'm already washed up, Lorraine." Then he turned away from me to Ramona. "You should come with Russ to the Lake Tavern this weekend. They have deep fried cheese curds."

Cheese curds? What a dope!

"Well, Kenny." I glared at the fool through my forced smile. "We have a meeting at school this week."

"I know, Lorraine." He glared right back at me.

What was I supposed to say? I wanted to tell Kenny he was a jerk to flirt with a woman he'd just met in the family home of his dead wife. I wanted to invite Ramona and Russ to go home and take Kenny with them. I wanted to go after Charity. Of course, I didn't. I couldn't keep an eye on the dope if I did. What I did was I put my thoughts of vet school farther back in the recesses of my mind and didn't say anything about it to Momma.

Finally, Momma had served up platters of oven-fried chicken, steaming bowls of mashed potatoes with caramel colored milk gravy, rolls, salad, corn on the cob, and peas. She nodded at Dad. He took a big breath. His face looked pained, but he continued like a good soldier in Momma's small but growing army.

"God of Abraham, Isaac, and Joseph..."

"Crap," I mumbled under my breath. It's serious when Momma includes the supporting cast of the Old Testament. She wanted something big.

Dad continued, "God of Abraham, Isaac, and Joseph, you have heard our prayers lo these many years and you have been faithful to answer our prayers as we have been faithful to you. Bless these young lives and strengthen them to keep your commandments and healthy suggestions..."

I opened my eyes and looked at Dad. He snuck a look at me too. His eyes were big. *Healthy suggestions? It sounds like a section of the Perkins over fifty-five menu.* Momma managed to glare at us with only one eye open. Even one stink eye must have made it clear Dad better keep to the script.

"Help us, men and women, to find love and companionship in the ways of your commandments and healthy suggestions. Bless this food to the use of our body and bless the hands that prepared it. Mighty is God and blessed are those who keep God's holy, irrevocable word. Amen."

The prayer shamed me. The meal was horrid. I barely stomached eating seconds. Momma and Ricky talked about recipes. Dad and Russ talked about the pros and cons of rebuilding the engine in the station wagon versus turning the whole monstrosity into a planter. I could see Dad making pencil sketches on his paper napkin. I pictured our station wagon roofless, filled with dirt and seeded with flowers and vegetables. Worse than that, Kenny and Ramona whispered and giggled together. Occasionally, Kenny spouted something he'd just learned from the child development expert, Ramona.

"Hey, Lorraine, Ramona said I was right. You've got to stop calling my son Little Man. His name is Kenny Allan Hollister Jr. She thinks, and I agree, we better all get used to calling him Allan. That's so he isn't confused with me."

"I don't think anyone would confuse Little Man—I mean Allan, with you." I chuckled and rolled my eyes. "He's cute and smart. Big contrast there."

"Well, do it anyway. Call my son Allan." Kenny speared another piece of chicken for himself and passed the platter to Ramona.

God damn it, to add insult to injury, Ramona took the last thigh. The only redeeming thing about the meal was Little Man kept jabbering, "I not Allan, I Little Man." And Momma announced she had just invited Ricky to move into one of the spare rooms in our upstairs. If I could ignore his sucking up to Momma, he could be a good friend. The queers in our house had doubled. I doubt Momma knew she had added to the enemy forces. I'd let her find that out for herself in her own sweet time.

Chapter Three

THE NEXT DAY I washed and dried the lions as Charity and "Allan" dipped hippos into the chocolate pudding watering hole. The elephants were in the dish drainer. My beast of a Momma tormented folks at the medical clinic, Dad and Kenny were at work at the lumber yard—Charity had joined me to play African jungle with Little Man. *Shit, I'm supposed to call him Allan.*

The day was muggy for being only June. The only cool spot was directly in front of a dusty oscillating fan in the kitchen or standing in front of the refrigerator with the door open. Momma didn't believe in air conditioning. She heard that people who were comfortable on a regular basis had a higher incidence of cancer.

I did my best to create a fun African scene. Charity had seemed mad at me the night before. I wanted her to have a good time with me and Little Man. *I mean Allan.* I'd placed every house plant and potted outdoor plant my momma owned in the kitchen. Stuffed animals flanked a homemade jungle. I'd lined up all Momma's cake pans including her sacred, giant cinnamon roll pan and filled them with chocolate pudding representing mud, butterscotch pudding representing the dry grassy plain, and vanilla pudding just because it tasted good. I'd wanted to dress in a loincloth, but I figured with my luck the church choir and Charity's minister dad would happen by and I'd have given them more ammunition to call me depraved.

I nuzzled next to Charity's ear.

Charity shrugged me off. "Raine, it's too hot."

Momma had given me strict orders: Little Man should not and would not witness any messing around. She didn't mention Charity specifically, but her meaning was clear. Keep my lust in my heart. Still, I had hopes for nap time and hadn't expected Charity to put me off. It wasn't like Little Man's head would explode if he witnessed us kissing. I don't think Little Man thought much about it. He liked to kiss everybody: Momma, Dad, all the dogs.

I tried a different approach. I stood behind Charity with my arms laced around her waist.

"Did you write them and tell them when you're coming?" Charity said as she turned to face me.

She looked hot, but her words made me shiver. I played dumb. "Who, where?"

Charity ducked out of my embrace. Her face got red and she put her hands on her wonderful hips. "You didn't contact the college yet?"

I knew darn well what she meant. I had received an acceptance letter for a college with a pre-veterinary science program and needed to decide once and for all on an entrance term—fall or spring or not at all. They had made it clear they would not defer my enrollment again. I'd put them off twice already: once when I lost my scholarship to go there because my own momma had told the holier-than-thou scholarship benefactor, McGerber, and Pastor Grind I was queer. I postponed once again, when I decided to stay home and care for my nephew, after my sister died and my momma went off to nursing school. A year had passed, and both the vet school and Charity were getting impatient.

"Can't we just keep playing Africa?" I whined and lowered my head, hoping my big brown cow eyes would charm her into letting the topic drop. I moved closer. I wanted to bury my face in the creamy pink skin of her neck. I wanted to touch and smell her auburn hair. "I'll show you my zebra if you show me yours." I don't even know what I meant. Bless her heart, Charity kissed me quickly on the lips but frowned at me.

"Show me your zebra," Little Man said.

"What difference does it make if I go this year or next? I'm doing the work I like with Twitch already without my degree, and we're going to come back to Bend anyway. You're doing your art. What difference does it make that I haven't left yet? We're going to end up back here anyway."

Silence.

Why isn't she saying anything?

"Charity, that's the plan, right?"

Charity didn't answer. She turned away from me, took a kitchen towel from the counter, and dried her hands.

I looked at Charity standing in my kitchen and goose bumps pattered up and down my arms and my nipples got scared hard. I saw her anew. Charity, unattainable again, older than me, more educated than me, more experienced than me. She'd already finished college. She'd had lovers before. What made me think our getting together could last? I may have made good grades in school, but I was pretty damn stupid.

"Raine, I want Grandpa in Africa." Little Man licked his fingers, but still had pudding up to his elbows. Little Man, Little Man, my drug. He saved me from feeling all the pain the world willingly heaped in my direction. I turned from staring at Charity.

"Kenny and your grandpa will love seeing your plastic animals in pudding. Your grandma, however, will blow a gasket."

"What's a gasket?" he asked.

"It's your grandma's biggest organ." My momma had no patience for messes—especially mine. She only tolerated messes she'd made herself, but she denied ever having made any.

"You know what I wish? I wish your mommy, Becky, could see you play with your plastic animals. She'd be so proud of you." I invoked the name of my dead sister like a shield against the world and today even against Charity. Who could possibly harangue me about anything when they thought about my poor sister? The invocation may have safeguarded me from questions from Charity, but it opened the door for other messy questions from Little Man. *Shit, I mean Allan.*

"Where's she at?" Allan galloped giraffes through the pudding and into the soapy water in the sink.

I looked at Charity again. She faced me with a sad smile. She knew because I'd told her often enough I hated this part of taking care of my nephew. There was no place to get away from the memories of my sister killing herself. I hated telling Li—*I'm supposed to call him Allan*—anything about his mommy's death.

"Your mommy was an angel from God. She was the most beautiful and smartest girl who ever lived in Bend, Minnesota." Saying those words would have gagged me before Becky died, but now they were just part of the scripted lie I told him every time he asked about her.

"Your daddy couldn't help but fall in love with her, marry her, and have a baby." I fudged the order of things when I told him the story. The truth is Becky and Kenny made a baby before they got married and before either of them graduated high school. "That baby, what's his name?"

"Little Man," he giggled.

"You're right. Your mommy loved you so much, she couldn't wait to go to heaven to tell Jesus thank you." I choked back tears every time I told this story.

The lie wasn't my idea. Pastor Allister Grind had advised Momma to tell the story to the boy. Momma never defied Allister Grind. He'd been Momma's love as a teen and Momma trusted anyone she thought had the inside track with God. I didn't trust Pastor Grind and I didn't honor all things he said because he hated queers and I was queer and secretly dating his queer daughter, Charity. However, on the topic of what to tell my nephew about the death of his momma, I followed his advice. No way I wanted to be the one to tell him how his momma really died.

He slipped off the kitchen chair, bent over stretching his arms out in front of him, and let the dogs finish cleaning the pudding off his hands and face.

After his canine tongue lashing, he pushed his overgrown bangs out of his eyes. "I'm taking the tractor to heaven." He made *vroom vroom* noises as he pulled trucks and cars out of his toy box looking for his green John Deere tractor Grandpa had given him.

My heart shattered every time the little fart said something sweet. His grief seemed more important than the ways Momma, Dad, Kenny, and I missed Becky. So what if my feet were nailed to the floor and I hadn't left yet? Allan had been robbed of a mother and was too young to have any memories of his own. It was my job to seed his mind with stories of Becky and fertilize the soil with the necessary embellishments. Some of the stories I planted happened and others should've happened or would've happened if Becky had lived and gotten well.

As long as I had Allan and Kenny with me at the farm, by God I was going to do everything in my power to give Allan the best childhood and the best memory of a mom who loved him. It was the least I could do, and it was the most I could do now Becky had died, and I failed to save her.

Charity and I began cleaning the kitchen.

Silence.

"I know you came to Bend against your will. You came here to protect Kelly from being fired and maybe prosecuted for being your lover at the same time she taught you art." I knew the risk of bringing up these old, but sensitive facts about the circumstances of Charity moving back to Bend.

Kelly had been an adjunct professor at Charity's college. The two became lovers. When they were discovered, Charity convinced the school it was better to tell her dad she'd be finishing her last few credits by correspondence rather than telling him a professor had been dating his daughter. Charity avoided being outed, the school dodged being disgraced or sued, and Kelly ducked prosecution.

Charity kept scrubbing the plastic animals.

I went on with my speech. "You didn't plan on meeting me and us getting together."

It would have been a fine time for Charity to say she wouldn't change a thing and meeting me was the best thing that ever happened to her. Charity didn't speak. She moved the animals to the rinse water.

What I couldn't bring myself to say is she had left Kelly for me. She had delayed art school in St. Paul. Sure, she completed some commissioned artwork in Bend and fattened her portfolio, but her dream had always been full-time art school in the city. Commuting back and forth to St. Paul like she'd been doing hadn't been her first choice, and it showed. I wished I could tell her I understood why her patience waned, but I didn't. I wanted her to wait for me and my own timing.

I put the stuffed animals and plants away, washed the pans, looked high and low for any remnants of pudding. After I dried my hands, I took Little Man into my arms. I twirled him in the air and kissed his face and head. Little Man, Allan, the big rock that changed the course of my stream, my life. I didn't have the drive to be anywhere else.

I had barely finished removing the remnants of pretend Africa from the creases and crevasses of the kitchen when I heard a vehicle barrel up the drive and park next to my truck.

Ben "Twitch" Twitchell was my Dad's best friend, current boss and my veterinarian mentor, boss, and friend. When Becky got sick, I had learned Twitch was our biological father. He owned the sperm that scrambled my momma's eggs. Momma and Twitch had gotten together briefly when Momma first moved to Bend before she met and fell in love with my dad. *I bet Momma doesn't have that little tidbit in her notebook of sins.*

Twitch entered the kitchen jabbering, gesturing, and searching our refrigerator for a cold beer, which he would not find because Momma hid them from my dad anytime he brought some beer in the house. At that moment a six-pack of Grain Belt rested in the colored rock of the fish tank confusing four goldfish and a guppy.

"Don't say no! You're going to want to say no, but I need you to say yes." Twitch yapped at me. "What's happening here?"

"Hey, Twitch, we just finished playing Africa with Little Man if you have to know," I said. "What do you want? It's my day off."

"Africa? Good. Say, I've got a little safari for you. Besides, if you aren't going to go to vet school you might as well play one at home. Hello, Charity." He bowed.

"Hey." Charity smiled at Twitch without enthusiasm. She probably thought if he weren't letting me work with him I would get my butt moving out of town.

"No wonder you're not married. You're a horrible salesman, Twitch," I said.

"Horrible salesman," Little Man repeated.

I had Little Man on my hip and the dogs were at my side, whipping my legs with their tails. I put Little Man—Allan—down on the kitchen floor. He ran to Twitch.

Twitch picked up the boy and swung him in the air nearly taking out the ceiling fan.

"Hello, big boy, how're you doing? Anybody give you a real name yet?"

He put the boy back on his feet. Little Man stumbled around dizzy.

"Last night Kenny made a declaration that Little Man is from this day forward to be known as Allan. So, his name is Allan. I just don't like using it."

"Hmm. You're stubborn just like your parents." Twitch blushed after he said it.

Allan looked over at me and mimicked Twitch, "You're stubborn."

Twitch laughed. "I could listen to this parrot all day, but there's work to do." He rubbed his hands together.

"You're right, Lorraine. I'm not good at sales, but I could become good at begging if needed. I just want you to know I wouldn't ask you to do this if I really didn't need you to promise me you will."

"Well, it looks like you two have plans," Charity said and headed for the door.

"Wait, I thought we were going to spend the day with Allan, and then go out by ourselves later," I said.

"It looks like Twitch needs you for something," Charity said. "I'm going home or maybe back to St. Paul."

Charity may have been smiling, but I saw the sadness in her eyes. Yet the easy way Charity let go of our plans bothered me. That discussion would need to happen privately another time. I knew Twitch still cringed at talk about me being queer.

"I'll call you later." I said the words to a slamming screen door. I turned to Twitch. "Okay, I'll do it as long as I am done by supper." I watched Charity speed out of our yard. She'd left without kissing me. I couldn't remember that ever happening since we got back together.

"You're still seeing that girl?" Twitch asked. "I thought she moved away."

"Yes, I'm still seeing Charity." I think Twitch enjoyed teasing me about stuff as much as I enjoyed razzing him. "Although, I haven't seen her much lately. I had planned to spend the night at her place tonight. So just tell me what you need me to do so I can get it over with."

"I need you to go over to McGerber's farm..." Twitch started.

"No way in hell!" I finished.

I turned away from Twitch and walked out onto the front porch letting the screen door slam behind me. The dust Charity had stirred up hung in the air. *Damn it. Why didn't I ask him the specifics before Charity left?* If I'd known he wanted me to go to McGerber's place, I would have said no and kept my plans with Charity.

Twitch had scooped up Little Man and followed me outside. The dogs raced out on his heels and chased after a squirrel in the yard.

The nerve of the man. Twitch of all people knew better than to ask me to ever step foot on J.C. McGerber's farm. I wanted absolutely nothing to do with J.C. McGerber. I paced, kicked at the dirt, and swore under my breath.

"If you're done with the Irish dancing, I'll tell you what I need you to do."

I flashed a look at him I hoped would register on a Geiger counter.

"Look Lorraine, the calf is already lost. If somebody who knows what they're doing doesn't get over there the cow is going to die too." He put a hand over one of Little Man's ears. "God damn it, Lorraine. That's why I asked you to promise me."

"God damp it!" Allan said.

"You do it." I went back into the house. Suddenly, being outside with him felt like the fires of hell. I let the screen door slam.

Twitch followed me into the house. "I would if I could, but I can't. McGerber won't let me on the place."

"Why not?"

Twitch glanced at Allan and whispered to me, "There's some unkind gossip making the rounds about some married ladies in town and a certain sensitive bachelor."

"Christ," I said as I took the boy out of Twitch's arms and put him down on the floor with a cookie.

"Christ," Allan said as he slapped his thigh with one hand and then took a bite of cookie. Never missing an opportunity for breaking bread with the messy toddler, the dogs had hightailed it back in the house and sat at Allan's feet watching for crumbs and ready to lick him clean.

I had to laugh. My sensitive bachelor, biological father had leanings toward affairs with married women. No surprise to me.

"Don't laugh. Those ladies had their reputations soiled by malicious busybodies." He shook his finger at me.

"What about your reputation?"

Twitch looked at me and rolled his eyes. "Hell! My reputation's shot already. Anyway, McGerber's on his high horse and won't let me on the place, but he has a contract with my vet service and as long as the work gets done, he still has to pay me." He kept looking at me waiting for me to say I'd do it for him.

When I didn't say anything, he tried again.

"Sorry, but since you don't have a date, you have plenty of time to see McGerber's cow."

"Thanks for your support, Twitch." My dating and disappointments didn't seem to count to Twitch or anybody else. I didn't want to deliver a calf and save a cow—well, I did, but I also wanted to brood. I had good reason: Charity broke our date and planned to leave town again. *What does it mean?* I worried she'd lost interest in the little town of Bend and her late-blooming-uneducated-girlfriend. *Me.* I still hoped she'd stay patient. Momma had finished her classes and began her clinicals at Bend's new medical clinic. I had completed two biology classes, anatomy, physiology, and plowed halfway through chemistry. Allan could start the new pre-school program for three to five-year-olds. I just needed a little more time to… I wasn't sure. I just needed a little more time and to leave on my own terms.

So, even though I didn't want to go to McGerber's farm, I said I would. The work would be a good distraction so I didn't have to think about losing Charity.

"I'll save the cow, but I hope I don't have to talk to the old fart."

"Just deliver the stuck calf and drench his sheep. He's probably not interested in conversation with you either."

"Damn. What about Little Man?" I asked.

"You mean Allan?" Twitch smiled.

"Damn!" Little Man shook his head. "What about Allan?"

"Kenny and Dad are at work at your lumber yard and Momma's at the clinic."

"I'll take him with me back to town to my office," Twitch said. "He can play with my hypodermic needles and wrestle a rabid coon I have in a cage. I'll look after him until your folks are free to get him."

"Sounds safe. Just don't visit any of those soiled ladies with Little Man along." I tied my hair back and corralled it under a hat.

"Soiled ladies," Allan said.

Twitch transferred a cardboard box from the back of his Jeep into the back of my beat-up pickup while I put on some work clothes and boots. I stuffed a couple of extra pairs of coveralls in the truck cab.

"The supplies you'll need are right there. McGerber has two hired hands. Lewis and Petey have worked on farms all over Minnesota. They know how to manage ornery critters—they'll help you with McGerber and that cow." He handed me a cardboard box of stuff. "Oh, try not to take all day!"

"Really?" I couldn't believe he had the nerve to ask me to step foot on McGerber's farm and also be quick about it. I transferred a car seat into the back of Twitch's Jeep and strapped in Allan. "Remember to remind him to use the bathroom. Sometimes he's playing so hard he forgets and pees where he stands."

"Sounds like me," Twitch said.

"Try not to tarnish any reputations in front of...Allan." I placed a backpack with a change of clothes, a banana, baggie of carrots, and some toys in the front seat of Twitch's Jeep.

Chapter Four

J.C. MCGERBER was slightly younger than God but had more money and an abundance of judgment. He farmed six hundred and forty acres and he owned around two hundred sheep and a hundred beef cattle. He had full-time hired hands all year round. His nails and clothes never got dirty and I doubted the man even sweated for himself. I imagined he regretted not having lived in the time of slavery so he could have legally owned some people. He had a slew of part-timers for haying, plowing, planting, and harvesting. I hadn't met any of them and didn't particularly care to meet any that day. I suspected they might be overly pious like McGerber and ready to condemn me for whatever sin they happened to notice about me.

The old man had a modest amount of new equipment. McGerber kept the buildings freshly painted, the fences mended, the grass and hedges trimmed and tidy probably because he had the money to pay someone else to do it. His place had what some called road appeal. By comparison our place screamed for attention. Unlike the holy man, Dad had to work at the lumber yard besides running the farm and we weren't wealthy. McGerber had none of the lawn ornaments and plastic animal tableaus which littered our farmyard because of Dad's tastes, sense of whimsy, and resolve to irritate Momma. McGerber's place flaunted its tidiness but looked naked and cold. Of course, I was biased. *I hate him.*

No one greeted me when I first arrived at McGerber's place, so I fiddled with the equipment Twitch had given me for the job. While bent over my kit digging out gloves, I didn't hear or see McGerber until he was right behind me.

"Miss Tyler."

Shit. I almost wet myself. All the rage and disappointment I felt when I dealt with him a few years back flooded to my mind and body. Immediately, I was transported back in time to the church office being told I'd lost the scholarship all over again. I tried my best to slow my breathing, but my face was flushed and my fists were clenched. McGerber didn't appear flapped at seeing me. He wasn't even sweating in the hot weather. Vampire. He looked even more self-righteous than I remembered.

When I stood up and faced him it surprised me to realize he was a fairly tall man. I'd basically only seen the back of his head at church. The day Pastor Grind called me to his office, McGerber was already seated. Back at the scholarship meeting he seemed to find great satisfaction in telling me he'd taken back the scholarship I'd won. He rescinded the scholarship because it had been reported to him, "Lorraine has unnatural desire." It was the same scholarship he hadn't awarded to Becky because she was pregnant our senior year. It meant nothing to him. He had taken away my hope at a future. Snatching back the scholarship seemed as easy and natural as dusting his church shoes.

Now Becky was dead, and I didn't need his scholarship money because I did vet work for Twitch. Momma and Dad had helped me save money too and given their blessing on a student loan if necessary. Still, I resented McGerber's part in our family's reversal of fortunes. Becky and I'd been the top students in our senior class and at least one of us should've had the money. I couldn't help thinking if Becky had won it, she might've gone to college and may have still been alive.

I looked at McGerber but bit my tongue. *I'm here to deliver a calf and vaccinate his sheep as a favor to Twitch. It's my job to service animals even if they were owned by people who hated me.* I didn't understand how my being queer hurt McGerber or was any of his business. I owed him the common courtesy I owed all people and nothing more, not even polite conversation. As I stood in silence, two men I'd never seen before came into the barn. The older one attempted a joke with the younger one.

"And he says, 'well, the only thing comes out of Kansas is steers and queers. Which one are you?'" Both men laughed.

Oh great.

McGerber laughed too as he stared at me. "Lewis, Pete, leave us a moment," he said without seeming to look at them. "I want to talk to Miss Tyler before she gets to work. We're old friends." He smiled, his teeth stained from coffee or cola probably. I doubted he smoked.

Hearing him say we were friends made my stomach cramp. I didn't want to be alone with him. I tried to hide my fear and disgust by going back to my prep work. *Crap. What if he attempts an exorcism?* Maybe he planned to kill me outright. I acted less shaken than I felt. At the same time, I wondered what thoughts had surfaced from McGerber's holy head. Maybe, he wanted to apologize. *Wow, the heat's getting to me.*

"I thought you were going to go to vet school. Certainly, you can't have finished it yet or did you drop out and follow the path of your uneducated parents?"

Oh, how he rankled me, but I would not use vulgarity or violence to match his already low estimation of me. "Oh, maybe you haven't heard about it. Momma's been attending college. She's going to be a nurse. Furthermore, I'm going to college too. I didn't drop out." I didn't bother to tell him why I stayed back a year. It was none of his business. "Twitch trained me enough to do what needs doing here."

"Well, we'll see," he said. He laced his hands behind his back and walked further into the barn. "I have the largest, most healthy flock of sheep in this entire county. Do you know why, Miss Tyler?"

"Probably because Twitch has been doctoring them and advising you on how to keep them healthy and productive." He'd never apologize. He'd only gloat. The very fact of it made me less afraid of him. He was tall from head to boot, but he was a small man.

"No, Miss Tyler. You're wrong, yet again. I have the largest, most healthy flock because I follow God's law and because I follow His law, He has blessed me. Deuteronomy chapter seven says if you pay attention to His laws He will keep His covenant of love with you. He will bless you. He will bless the fruit of your womb, the crops of your land—your grain, new wine and oil—the calves of your herds and the lambs of your flocks." He waved his arm around motioning to his large farm. "I prosper because God has blessed me. Do you understand, Miss Tyler?"

My mind raced with the things I wanted to say and could say but shouldn't say. Those weren't nice things and saying them would get me kicked off the place and Twitch wouldn't get paid. *I mustn't cross a line that hurts my family.* I chose my words carefully and kept a cheerful tone.

"You sure do have nice herds and flocks and I hear you have plenty of people to care for them for you. You don't have a womb. And it is my understanding your seed didn't produce any fruit in your wife's womb. Maybe you meant Fruit of the Loom and God blessed your underwear." He didn't seem too mad. I grew a little bolder. I stepped closer to the creep. "To tell you the truth, Mister McGerber, I'm not here to talk theology with you or how rich people think their wealth is a sign of their holiness and their opportunity is a sign of their superiority over those with fewer opportunities. I'm here to deliver a stuck calf, plain and simple."

"It is plain, but not so simple. I have a contract with the vet service and I'll honor it, but I will not have an adulterer on my property. Transgressors must be punished and will be punished by God with the assistance of the godly. I don't like the idea of having you and your unnatural ways on my land either. I let you serve me because you're young and there's still a chance you'll recognize the error of your ways. However, make no mistake, Lorraine, I will not renew the contract next year and I will advise all the farmers in the Sheep and Cattleman Association to do the same. That, you can count on."

"I'm guessing Twitch constructed the contract. If it had been you, you'd have had a morality clause, so you could get out of it."

"You are correct for once, Miss Tyler."

"Are you perfect, Mister McGerber?" I said. I don't know what gave me the courage to ask such a question.

"Excuse me, Miss Tyler?"

"I asked if you were perfect."

"All have sinned and fallen short of the glory of God," he said. "I take my instruction from scripture and, of course, the spiritual guidance of Pastor Grind."

"I take it you mean you're not perfect either. Good to know."

He turned around and left the barn.

My knees shook. My jaw ached from clenching it. My body had kept score of years of anger, disappointment, hate, and fear. I couldn't let go of it with a couple of deep breaths and stretches. I kicked hay bales. I screamed into my elbow. I shook out my arms and rotated my neck to let the scared energy leave me. As I stood there staring off into the neatly stacked hay and clean floors, I saw a blonde head pop up from behind a bale.

"What? Wait...who are you?" I called. I worried I'd begun seeing things that weren't there. Then, a slip of a girl in a baggy dress came out from behind the hay.

"I'm Addie," she said.

She came over to me and peered into my box of supplies.

"Are you visiting McGerber?" McGerber didn't have any children of his own to my knowledge.

"No. I have to live with him. He's fostering me. My social worker says my mom's not fit."

She didn't seem too bothered by what she said. She knelt by my box of supplies and pulled out items, reading labels and shaking the bottles.

"Oh, well, I'm sorry your mom's not fit and even sorrier you have to live with that..." I tried to think of something other than a swear. "Old fart."

She laughed. "He's a self-righteous asshole, but he's okay. I know what he expects from me." She stood up, put her hands on her hips. "Are you some sort of vet?"

"Yes, well almost," I said. "I still have to go to vet school, but I apprentice with Twitch, the local vet, and I know how to do a lot of things." She looked about fourteen, but she could have been older. Her dress hung loosely on her thin frame, disguising her figure. Her hair was long, clean, and tied away from her face with a ribbon which complimented her dress. She fidgeted. Before I could ask her questions about her living with McGerber, she skittered toward the door, picked up a gunny sack, stopped, and looked back at me.

"Well, almost vet, I have to go," she said. "I'm supposed to drown a litter of barn kittens."

"Drown kittens? Wait." I walked closer to her, looked around for McGerber. I whispered, "He's got you drowning kittens?"

Addie stepped closer to me. In hushed tones, she explained her predicament. "He says a whore of a barn cat had another litter and he would be damned if it would fall upon him to feed them. I suspect the cat's unmarried, which makes it fornication. Or, maybe she's married. That makes it adultery. Whatever sin it is, he don't abide it. He says the world already has too many strays. He don't abide strays, except for me, I guess. He gave me this sack." She held up a gunny sack.

Jesus Christ on a bicycle. "Do you want to drown kittens, Addie?"

"No, would you?" She frowned and looked at her feet.

I wondered how many similar decisions she'd faced in her short life. How could she consider drowning babies?

"They're so little and cute. It's not their fault they were brought into this unfit world."

"No, it's not their fault and it isn't the momma cat's fault either." I thought for a minute. I was there to deliver a stuck calf and drench some sheep, but there wasn't anything to say I couldn't also save some kittens and save a poor, young girl from being an instrument of death. "Do you think you can catch them all and the momma cat too?"

"Yes, she's used to me now because I give her my leftover breakfast cereal milk and the little ones are in a nest with her."

I walked back to my gear, dumped my equipment out on the floor, and handed the empty box to Addie.

"Sometimes, new mommas need some help to care for their babies especially when they weren't planned and when the momma isn't very grown herself."

Addie took the box from me. She looked confused.

"Put the momma cat and all those kittens in this box. Cover the box with the bag he gave you. Then put the box on the floor in my pickup, it's the old blue one out front. You'll have to go through the driver's door because the passenger door doesn't open from the outside. Oh, and crack the window open, it's so hot."

She nodded and took the box.

"Don't tell McGerber—just say you got rid of the kitties."

"Are you going to drown them?"

Her question shocked me, but I guess I shouldn't have expected her to know all the options. "No, I'm not going to kill them. I'll take them home to our barn. I can spay the momma cat so she doesn't have any more litters. She can focus on those kittens. They'll be okay. Maybe you can visit them some time. And when they're old enough to leave their momma, you can have one of them for your own."

"Maybe she likes having kittens. Anyway, how can you take them? They're his."

"They aren't important to him if he wanted you to kill them. He won't miss them."

"I wouldn't be too sure. He says it's his right to do what he wants with what he owns and whatever is an abomination to God. I bet he includes strays he thinks need to be killed. Believe me he knows what he owns."

"McGerber doesn't own everything just because it ends up on his farm. I'm saving those kittens if you'll help me."

"Okay, I guess if you're an almost vet you know what you're doing. I'm just a girl with an unfit mother and an old fart foster dad."

Somehow, I suspected Addie had more going for her than she let on.

Then the two farmhands returned. The older one took a last drag on a cigarette and snubbed it out on the barn floor and shoved a stick of chewing gum in his mouth. "McGerber said take you to the cow and do whatever you tell us to do. I'm Lewis Gaus and this young man is my good friend, Petey Holman—he's harmless unless you date him." The older one, Lewis, put the younger man, Petey, in a headlock. Petey fought out of the hold and punched Lewis in the shoulder.

"Shut up, Lewis!" Petey ran his hands through his mussed hair.

Addie smiled and waved as she left the barn.

Cautiously, I stepped forward. After that queer remark earlier, I was halfway determined not to like them, but Twitch had said they were okay. I gave them a chance. I shook hands with the two men. Lewis was tall, muscled, and hairy. His full beard and bushy mustache gave way to wavy hair falling on his collar and held back by a well-worn cowboy hat. Petey was a husky young man with silver hair that didn't match his age or first impression. When he smiled, I could easily imagine what he looked like when he was four years old—no gray hair, but the same boyish face.

"Come join us at the shit show," Lewis said.

I followed them to the cattle barn. If Twitch hadn't already warned me McGerber and his men had made a grisly failed effort to deliver the calf, I would've puked at what I found. The cow was down on her side, breathing shallowly and in obvious distress. A bloody stump of neck protruded from her vagina. A vacant-eyed calf head lay on the floor. They had tried to pull the calf out with a chain and decapitated it. The rest of the calf was hidden, stuck inside the suffering cow.

"What a mess!" I didn't intend to make them feel any worse, but it needed to be said. "Come on, let's get this cow out of her misery."

I had left the supplies for drenching the sheep back at the barn where I unloaded my box and gave it to Addie for the kittens. The rest of the equipment I had bundled in my arms and carried to the cow barn. Again, I inventoried what Twitch had sent with me for the job.

First, I needed to perk up the cow. I shot her up with a pint of 50 percent dextrose. Then I gave her a spinal epidural, so she would stop straining and be still enough for me to reach inside her, reposition the dead calf, and deliver it. I mixed up an iodine solution as a disinfectant. I'd seen Twitch reposition calves at least a half-dozen times and done it myself twice.

"Will you look at that," I said into the supplies. "Damn if that man isn't smart." Twitch had sent a box of laundry soap.

"What're you talking about?" Lewis kneeled by me.

"The soap." I nodded at the box.

"I get it, you're going to soap up the calf and slide it out," Lewis said. "Lookie here, Petey." He showed the box to Petey. "Petey's only a pup—barely eighteen. He's seen a lot of things on the farms we've worked, but I doubt he's seen miracle bubbles."

I unzipped my coveralls and took my arms out of the sleeves and let the top hang at my waist. I covered my hand and arm with a plastic glove that extended to the shoulder of my sleeveless T-shirt. Once I'd lowered myself on the hay behind the heifer, the headless neck of the calf was right in my face. Flies buzzed by it and landed on it, probably laying their maggot eggs. I sprinkled the laundry soap on my gloved hand.

"Here goes nothing." I reached inside the cow. The moisture dissolved the soap into a lather I spread wherever I could reach. I smelled blood, piss, and shit, but concentrated on what I'd been taught. The book drawings of the cow insides flashed in my head as I fished around and read the situation with my hand.

"The calf's shoulders are locked up at the cow's pelvis." I nodded at Petey. "Help me get another glove on and soap it up good."

He knelt beside me and followed my every instruction.

"I'm sorry to be intruding on you this way, Miss Cow, but I promise you will feel better once I get your baby out."

Finally, I had lubricated the area enough that I could rotate the calf and free it. I soaped it as I turned it. My gloved hands and arms were slick with soap, blood, and mucus. The rest of me was soaked with sweat like I'd run to get there, but eventually, the calf slipped out.

"Well, I'll be damned! That's impressive, Miss Tyler. Petey and I'll take it from here and clean her up."

"Good work for a queer?"

"Well, I don't know what to say about that, Miss Tyler." Lewis spit chewing tobacco on the floor. "I guess it was good work no matter what you are."

"Call me Lorraine."

"Damn fine work, Lorraine." Petey shook my hand again.

I didn't know if my challenge made a difference or just made Lewis hate queers more. I'd grown tired of letting all the jokes and stupid comments go by.

The men each grabbed a pair of gloves when I pointed to the box. The cow wasn't torn up inside as best as I could tell. I left them to their work and went to the wash area in the entry of the barn, discarded my dirty gloves, and washed my hands and arms. Then I got a clean set of coveralls from my truck and put them on over my jeans and T-shirt. I heard a faint mewing from the passenger side when I opened the driver's door and stuffed my dirty clothes in a garbage bag from the glove box. Addie had gotten the stray kittens and their momma captured and stowed them in my truck. So far, I'd saved a cow and litter of kittens. Not bad for an almost vet—a queer almost vet, I might add.

The drenching equipment was in the sheep barn where I left it. The sheep had been separated into holding pens which made it easy for me to begin drenching them without the help of Lewis and Petey. The men came along in short order and seemed downright friendly to me since they'd seen me pull that calf out. The event made me some sort of magician to them now, or at least a competent vet's assistant.

They kept a steady line of sheep coming to me to be drenched and then penned them separate from the ones we hadn't drenched yet. I planned to do the whole flock that day, so I didn't have to worry about Lewis and Petey keeping the "haves" from the "have nots."

"How long you been working for Twitchell?" Lewis asked.

"Since high school really," I said. "I am accepted at vet school. I just got to get myself going there."

"Well, I suppose there's more they could teach you, but you seem to know a lot already," Lewis said.

I didn't yet know if I liked Lewis or not, but I could work with him.

After only about a third of the flock had been vaccinated, McGerber materialized again and interrupted.

"I hate to interrupt," he said.

"Then don't," I said.

"There's a matter of some importance that needs your attention, that is if you really are a vet." He glared at me.

Bait! I knew it, but I took it anyway. "What's so important you're interrupting my work?"

"It seems I have a bull whose horns are unsafe."

Petey groaned and Lewis spit on the floor by his boots.

"You want me to stop drenching your sheep to dehorn your bull?" *Did the man thrill to pissing me off or was he trying to weasel out of his contract?* I didn't care. I hadn't backed down to him or his hired help. I saved a cow and I'd thwarted McGerber's attempt to kill a litter of kittens. Call me Supervet! Bring on the horny bull.

"Yes. Is that a problem, Miss Tyler? Maybe it's beyond your abilities."

Ooh, the man is a masochist hungry for a beating or I am. Either way, I'm not leaving.

"No. I'll wash up and get some gear from the truck." I'd like to have put that gunny sack over McGerber and drowned him.

"Killer is in the north barn." McGerber walked out.

"Killer?" I squinted at Lewis and Petey. "He's got a bull calf already named Killer?"

"Killer's not a young calf," Lewis said. "He's a full-grown bull and he's a son of a bitch! Come on, we'll show you the devil spawn." Lewis and Petey led me to Killer's pen.

My heart raced, and my throat felt tight. I wished I had Twitch with me or my dad.

Cattle are usually dehorned young and if the cutting or burning is done right, the horns don't grow back. Killer was five years old and over a ton of ornery muscle. His horns were a foot long—one had fault lines and cracks and came to a rounded nub and the other horn came to a point so Killer could have roasted wieners and marshmallows by the fire. From the looks of him he preferred a vet assistant shish kebob.

Petey got a big rope around Killer's neck and Lewis tied it to a ring on the wall of the barn while I skinned off my coveralls.

"Are you sure you want to try this?" Lewis asked.

Hell no. "Nobody, especially not J.C. McGerber, is going to tell me what I can and cannot do."

Lewis put a line through Killer's nose ring, but left it loose so that he didn't pull his nose ring out if he panicked right away. Petey secured the big neck rope and held the bull's head steady. So far, he cooperated, and I wondered if he got his nickname unjustly or maybe McGerber had a penchant for irony.

I injected some painkiller into the nerves at the base of the horns. After a few minutes it took effect and I positioned the horn lopper—a tool like a giant bolt cutter—on the horn.

Thankfully, Petey and Lewis didn't expect me to prove I could lop those horns off all by myself. Petey held the big rope looped around Killer's neck and Lewis and I worked together with the lopper. We cut off the first horn. I laughed at the relief and ease of it, but Killer pulled loose from Petey and pulled the ring securing his rope right out of the wall board.

Oh shit!

Killer the unicorn bull was loose. Everybody scrambled in different directions, but Killer followed me. I ran toward the manure spreader and dashed to the other end of the barn in time to see the end door slide shut. What the heck? McGerber? Why would he close the door? Maybe killing my dreams a few years back didn't satisfy him enough. Now he'd kill me outright.

I darted to the right around a barn post and Killer made the same turn, but not as precisely. Whether it was the painkiller or just a lack of agility, I couldn't be certain, but Killer hit the barn post head on. Hay chaff filtered down like snow from hay mow and Killer fell unconscious to the floor. Petey raced over with the loppers. He and I cut off the other horn. I tossed the pointy horn at Lewis's feet a minute or two later when he joined us by the sleeping beast.

"Give those horns to McGerber. Tell him he knows where he can put them."

I put blood stopper powder on both stumps, gathered up the equipment, and got in my truck shaking so bad I wasn't certain I could drive. McGerber stepped into the lane, waved his arms, and blocked my way as I drove away from the barn. I resisted a strong desire to park my truck on McGerber's chest. I stopped inches from his toes, threw my dirty coveralls over the box of cats, and rolled down my window.

"What?"

"Well, Miss Tyler, have you finished drenching the sheep?"

"That's it for today. I'll be back tomorrow to finish the drenching with Petey and Lewis." I rolled up my window and hit the accelerator before he had time to impress me with his approval or disapproval.

The half-hour drive from McGerber's farm to ours gave me time to think and fume. I trembled, but I was proud too. So proud and sure of myself that I lengthened the trip by driving by Grind's place to check for Charity's truck. No truck. No Charity. I doubted she was waiting at the farm for me.

I drove through Bend. Boys scrimmaged on the high school's football field. Sanctioned, preseason practices were at least a month out, but a few guys played informally. When real practices begin, there'd be the crash of helmet to helmet and helmet to pads cracking like horned animals defending their turf. I blushed even as I noticed the closed-up concession stand. On one of the times Momma had ordered me to chaperone Becky and Kenny I'd been an accidental spectator to their lovemaking. Maybe Little Man was conceived that day. Maybe I'd seen something holy.

I continued through downtown. There were a few cars in town, none I recognized or cared enough about to find the drivers. No sign of Twitch. Hopefully he'd taken Allan home to Momma. Dad and Kenny were off work and probably at home. I headed that way myself.

When I got back home I released the contraband cats into the barn. The momma cat led her babies to hay where she would make a cozy nest for them. Allan would have a seizure when I showed them to him later. He'd call them "titties."

I called Twitch on my cell phone and left a message on his voicemail saying I had to go back tomorrow and finish drenching the sheep because McGerber interrupted my work to dehorn Killer. I hoped it riled Twitch some and made him never ask me to go to McGerber's place again.

I reviewed my priorities: find Momma, make sure she had Allan, and tell her what had happened at McGerber's place. On the heels of that I planned to break the news that I intended to write to the college and enter pre-veterinary classes as soon as arrangements could be made to take care of Allan. I wouldn't tell Momma I was panicked if I didn't leave for vet school soon I'd lose Charity.

Chapter Five

THE FOLLOWING DAY I reluctantly returned to McGerber's farm to finish drenching his sheep. My stomach clenched and I threw up yellow bile. I guess a near death experience will do that to you. I expected McGerber to pop up or the bull to finish what he'd started. It helped that Petey and Lewis were there when I arrived and McGerber was nowhere in sight. Petey, Lewis, and I drenched the rest of McGerber's sheep. The sheep were protected from worms, but they were still owned by one.

In celebration of our completed task and brief association Lewis had brought a six-pack of Coors beer in a cooler. I didn't care much for the taste of beer but joined them anyway. Had I ever in my life sat on the tailgate of a pickup drinking beer with two men? No, I hadn't, but there we sat in the back of Lewis's battered, dark green Ford truck. To me the beer lacked flavor, but the sweet thought that our beer drinking would probably irritate McGerber helped me finish the can I'd started.

"This is our last day working for the old man too," said Lewis. "I don't think he'll throw us any going-away party though. He's been flitting around like a mother hen. He said his brother's here for a while."

"I didn't know McGerber had a brother," I said. "He seems a one of a kind—a broke the mold sort of thing."

"I haven't met him, but McGerber bragged that his brother—Ward, or Ralph? Anyway, he's some sort of bigwig or other. Wears a suit and struts about." He rolled his eyes. "I'm not sure what he's talking about. That brother is around here some place, but I wouldn't know him from Adam other than he's about the same size as McGerber."

"I don't feel good that those guys are going to be here with..."

Before Petey could finish his sentence, Twitch came barreling up the drive in his Jeep. No surprise. He must've gotten the message on his office phone the night before. I didn't exactly lie or anything, but I may have said that McGerber tried to kill me by closing the barn door and blocking my escape from Killer the bull.

Twitch's Jeep had barely come to a stop before he leaped out of it and asking after McGerber.

"Where's the son of a bitch?" Twitch's face was flushed.

"This should be good," Lewis said to Petey. "Nothing's as fun as watching a good beating."

Twitch didn't have to go searching. McGerber flew out of the house and across the yard, through his white picket fence gate. He moved one gear slower than the vicious bull ran after me the day before.

"You have no business here," he said, waving his arms and shaking his finger. "I don't want you on my property, Twitchell. I'm busy. My brother Warren is here, and I have..." McGerber stopped speaking as the tow-headed waifish girl, Addie, came up beside him. She smiled in the direction of Petey, Lewis, and me. She wrung her hands as she fidgeted with the tent of a dress she wore.

Twitch stood his ground and stood toe-to-toe with McGerber.

"I don't give a flying"—Twitch glimpsed me and Addie—"I don't give a flying fig whether you want me here. Did you tell Lorraine to dehorn that maniac bull of yours?"

"Well, it needed to be done. Now you get off..."

McGerber hit the ground and I swear I never saw the punch that dropped him. He grasped his jaw with one hand and leaned on his elbow in the gravel drive. His gray comb-over flopped across his reddened face until he swept the oily hair back in place. He stayed down but yelled from the ground.

"Lewis, Petey, you saw what he did. Call the sheriff. This man assaulted me!"

Addie had flinched and covered her mouth with her hands, but she quickly knelt by McGerber.

Petey and Lewis slipped off the tailgate and put their empties in the case.

"I'm a spectator, but never a witness. Looked to me like you fell," Lewis said. "Probably your age. Careful you don't break a hip."

Petey tipped his hat to Addie while McGerber remained on the ground. Petey and Lewis got in Lewis's truck. Petey waved the bull horns at me as they drove out of the yard.

"I'll mail you your bill and I suggest you send your check promptly." Twitch stood over McGerber. "If I have to come out to get it I'll bring Lorraine's dad with me and you can bet he won't stop by punching you once. Hell, he'll probably shoot your head off with his shotgun."

"How dare you threaten me," McGerber said.

"I'm not threatening you. I'm giving you fair warning that when you endanger this young woman for your sick self-righteous amusement you're inviting wrath you cannot fathom. Hell, if I told her momma she'd kill you with her bare hands."

Twitch waited as I gathered my gear and packed it in my truck. I drove out of the yard. In the rearview mirror I saw Addie lean over to help McGerber stand. She dusted him off. McGerber put an arm around Addie's shoulders as she helped him walk to the house as dust distorted my view. *What is that old self-righteous fart doing with a high school girl living in his house?*

Chapter Six

"MAKE YOURSELF AVAILABLE, Lorraine. Ricky is moving into the north bedroom this Saturday." Momma had bought new towels. Wow, who knew it took a guest to add something new in the house? The old towels were so worn they were more exfoliant than comfy.

I waited on the front porch with the dogs as Ricky drove his little Honda into the yard on moving day. That car must have been like one of those magic clown cars. I couldn't believe the number of boxes he had. He owned more hair products, creams, and lotions than the entire nonperishable aisle of the grocery store.

Momma told him she'd made up a bedroom for him upstairs and he'd know which one. Christ, she'd put cowboy sheets on his bed and a poster with Betty Crocker's recommended spices for various cuts of meat.

I helped him carry his boxes upstairs.

He talked the whole time. "Lorraine, once I get my room organized I can start working on your hair."

Not going to happen.

"Oh, I can't wait to cook with your momma."

What a suck-up.

Ricky fiddled with bottles of nail polish, shaking them and holding them up to the light. "Your dad, which do you think he'd prefer? A pedicure or manicure or maybe both?"

He'd rather be poked in the eye than be fussed over.

"Dad's not the manicure, pedicure type of man. He cleans his fingernails with a jackknife and cuts his toenails with tin snips."

"People can change, Lorraine. Sometimes, they just need someone to pamper them and then they discover they like it and want to pamper themselves. That's business for me."

"Well, I understand your business plan, but I don't see this family as being very good customers."

Wrong again. I may not have been interested in his potions and poking and other cosmetic pursuits, but Ricky had barely lived with us for a week before he had convinced Momma, Dad, and Allan to have manicures, pedicures, and let him play with their hair. It felt like Ricky fit in our family and we'd found just the piece we'd been missing. Ricky, the daughter my mother never had, or at least he more closely resembled the daughter my momma missed. I told him his efforts were wasted on me, but it was just the thing Becky would have loved.

"My sister Becky could do hair. She helped me with mine sometimes. We played what we called 'beauty school drop-out,' no offense intended."

"None taken, Lorraine."

"I'm just saying she knew how to do all this stuff. She razzed me that I wasn't good at beautifying myself. Sisters fight I guess. Do you have any brothers or sisters, Ricky?"

"No, it's just me and my parents—well, and Marlene."

"Who's Marlene?"

"My girlfriend."

Yeah, right. And I'm keeping a stud for myself in the barn.

He pulled out his wallet and showed me a picture of a raven-haired Hispanic looking woman. "This is Marlene. She's away right now."

She's away all right. That picture probably came with your wallet. I didn't say anything, but it explained why maybe Momma coaxed Ricky to meet me. He claimed he and Marlene were engaged.

Marlene didn't come over or call and he didn't even pretend to call her.

But I hadn't seen Charity since the day we'd played Africa in the kitchen. Perhaps she had been eaten by cannibals or had only been in my fantasy like a picture that came with a new wallet. When I called Charity's cell phone it went right immediately to voicemail. She didn't answer my texts or respond to my attempts at emoji humor. I tried hearts, cute little chickens, and even lips. No response. It made me feel like that steaming poop emoji.

I mustered the courage to call the landline at the Grind house. Thankfully, Mrs. Grind and not Pastor Grind answered. Mrs. Grind told me Charity went back to the city for some art project or some class, or painting trip. I didn't believe it. I suspected Charity'd left for a naked orgy with beautiful college graduates who were able to leave behind their hometowns and nephews. At least her absence helped me have time to study. I worked ahead in every class and added a correspondence class in farm animal epidemiology.

Still, each time my newly acquired cell phone rang I hoped it was Charity, but invariably, it was Momma. She had at one time eschewed cell phones but became infinitely fascinated when I got one. She got one herself, but left it turned off most of the time to save the battery. She turned it back on to call me every couple of hours with a request or admonishment. Momma threatened to get one for Dad, but he told her if she did it would be a waste of good money. He'd either leave it sitting at home or throw it in the manure spreader or wood chipper. Most days after her third or fourth call I turned off my phone too. Technology is dangerous in the hands of the controlling. After so much hopeless waiting for a call from Charity I was willing to risk missing a call if it meant I could avoid the annoyance of another call from Momma. Ricky chewed me out for not answering his texts. "What if I had an emergency and needed you?"

Despite the number of times I swatted him away, he insisted on examining my hair and skin and made copious lists of products he thought I needed.

Fat chance.

Ricky eventually wore me down and I let him come into my room and see my "products" as he called them and peruse my closet of clothes. He tuned the radio in my radio alarm clock to KDWB and sang along to the music and danced some. His cologne smelled of musk and a hint of citrus. It was nice.

"You can call me Raine if you want. Charity calls me that."

"Raine, that's a sexy name." His eyes were deep brown, but tender like deer eyes.

I asked him questions while he sorted my clothes: one pile for clothes that could be cute and the other pile for the clothes I shouldn't be caught dead in. The latter pile quadrupled the former.

"Did your folks have a problem with you being a man who liked cosmetology?" Indirectly I wanted to ask him about which sexual orientation team he bowled on. We had talked a lot, but I hadn't yet asked him the big questions. It would make it a whole lot easier if I got that business out of the way. He'd know I didn't think of him as a boyfriend and we could both talk about our crushes or lovers or whatever the case might be. I badly needed somebody to talk to about my disintegrating relationship with Charity.

Ricky had put my clothes back in the closet, made a list of "essential wardrobe pieces" I needed to buy. He examined my current "products," a two in one shampoo and conditioner and a stick deodorant, and jotted down more products. He sat by me on the bed, took my hand, and shook his head at my jagged, short fingernails.

"I mean, there's nothing wrong with it in my book. My folks are okay with me wanting to be a vet, but my momma's ass is chapped that I'm queer. You know I'm queer, right? My girlfriend Charity's away a lot in St. Paul doing art."

"Oh yeah, I know. Kenny told us."

"Kenny told you?" *The turd. That's mine. It wasn't his to tell.*

"Sure, he told Russ, Melvin, and me. I don't think he wanted us asking you out."

"That jerk! I'm going to punch Kenny when he gets home and then I might poison him as well."

"I wanted to meet you. Your momma turned purple like she'd thrown an embolism or a brain aneurism every time she mentioned you. I had to see for myself. Besides, I like your momma. Her hair has a lot of body. Now, I like you too and I love your curls. May I?" He took a brush from his toolbox, lowered his head entreating me to trust him.

I nodded, and Ricky began brushing my curls—a useless exercise in my experience, but it felt nice. His touch was gentle, but also firm and confident.

"I think your momma hates the thought of unmarried children not living with parents."

"It's probably because of my sister, Becky. You know about Becky?"

"Yeah, your momma told me Becky was sick and died. Your momma cried when she talked about it and then she changed the subject to how I might like to meet you." Ricky stopped brushing my hair.

"Did you really see her die?"

"Yeah." I swallowed hard. *I heard telling the story would make it easier. Bullshit. Nothing makes it easier.* "It was horrible. Becky got ill. She'd always been spiritual, but in her illness, she got really confused. She wasn't a bad person, Ricky." *How could I ever explain to anyone?*

"Your sister got sick in her head?" He pointed his index finger at his head and rotated his hand at the wrist—the universal sign for crazy.

"She thought...she thought God wanted her to kill Little Man. She thought God told her to sacrifice Little Man to please God."

"Oh my God." Ricky put down the hairbrush. He knelt on the floor in front of me, gazing into my eyes and holding my hand.

I was right there in those woods again seeing it like a movie. "Becky got everything ready. She'd planned it. She piled up dead branches and she had a can of gasoline with her and a knife." Sloppy tears flooded my eyes. I'd never said the story out loud to anyone. I had just replayed it in my head day and night.

"I found her before she hurt anyone. I tried to get her to listen, but she wouldn't listen to me. She said she could hear God. That's why she didn't like the meds. She said when she took the medications she couldn't hear God's voice. She could hear God that day. She thought she could. She said God wanted a perfect sacrifice. I told her I would find a lamb for her sacrifice. We had sheep in that pasture. I could have caught one, but she wouldn't wait. She didn't want any substitute I found."

"What happened?" Ricky dabbed at my tears with the neatly pressed handkerchief he always kept in his back pocket. It smelled like his cologne.

"She doused the dry wood with gasoline and started a fire. Little Man slept on a blanket right by Becky's altar. I couldn't let her hurt Little Man—damn, I'm supposed to call him Allan. I refuse to call him Kenny Junior." I glanced at Ricky and wondered for a split-second what he'd think of me when I told him all of it. "I pushed her down, Ricky. I pushed Becky down and I snatched Allan away. I got him to safety."

"You were very brave."

"It didn't feel that way. I just did what I had to do, what anybody'd probably do if they saw a child in harm's way. But I didn't save Becky."

"What happened to Becky?" He got off the floor and sat next to me on the bed again.

"That's the part I can't get out of my head. I can't get free. Becky, Becky...I never dreamed Becky would do what she did next. She'd hurt herself before when she got sick, I didn't know about that except our neighbor, Gerry, saw her beat and whip herself. That's how we found out she was ill. I just never could have imagined... Ricky, Becky dowsed herself with the gasoline. She lifted that can above her head like it weighed nothing. She closed her eyes and let the gas soak her beautiful blonde hair and this dress she had I always liked. You'd have put that dress in the cute pile—white eyelet lace, cotton, sleeveless, very summery. The gas drooped her hair and stained her beautiful dress. She dropped the gas can to the side. She still had the knife."

The pleasant smell of Ricky's cologne evaporated from the room. I smelled gasoline like I did that day.

"She held the knife out in front of her with two hands. She glanced at me and then at the heavens. Then she pulled that knife into herself. Becky gasped. More stains on her pretty dress. She stabbed herself and dropped into the fire." I turned to face Ricky. "How could anybody do that?"

I'd never told anybody else, not even Charity. "I still see it in my dreams. I fought sleep for months but gave up. Being awake is just as bad." I grasped his hands in mine and stared straight into his eyes. "Ricky, I hear Becky's screams and I still smell her burning flesh. The whole scene, every day, rattles around in my head like an obnoxious tune."

Ricky grabbed me in a hug.

I let him.

"I'm sorry, Lorraine. Nobody should have to go through something so horrible. I'd rather die myself than see someone I love hurt so violently." He rocked me as I cried and snotted onto his shoulder and neck. He didn't let go and neither did I.

We stayed that way. I don't know for how long. When he let me go I noticed Ricky sobbed too. "I can't imagine losing someone like that and she was your twin?" He brushed the hair away from my face and I dabbed at his tears with my shirt sleeve.

"Weird, isn't it? Weird to think there is a sort of double of you out there. Don't get me wrong, Becky and I weren't much alike. We weren't identical twins by any stretch of the imagination. We fought more than we did anything, but no matter how much we fought or how different we were in the things we wanted, I didn't want her to die."

"Of course, you didn't want her to die."

I shuddered, suddenly exhausted. I fell back on the bed and wiped my nose and eyes. "Hey, I can't talk about loss anymore."

Ricky fell back on the bed next to me. I wished Momma would walk by just then. It would have pleased her to see me in bed with a man. I tried to compose myself. I rubbed my face, took my mint lip balm out of my pocket and brought it to my nose—anything to not remember the smell of that fire. I changed the subject.

"Ricky, do you have a boyfriend?" Hell, if I could talk about Becky I shouldn't have any qualms about asking Ricky anything.

Ricky blushed. "No. Not yet. Dad said he'd kill me and any boyfriend he catches. I believe him." His eyes widened.

"Is your dad religious?"

"No. He thinks religion is for stupid people." Ricky hopped up and began placing his beauty supplies back in his toolbox. "I hope I didn't offend you."

"No, I think there are a lot of stupid religious people too—not all of them, of course. I believe in God. I just think there are some people who twist what they know about God to justify doing some hateful things."

"My mom prays for me at her church. She's Catholic. She sends me money sometimes, when she can."

"How'd your parents find out you were queer?"

"I'm a cliché, Raine." Ricky leaned into my shoulder. "I don't want to kiss girls. I want to do their hair and makeup, gossip with them, stare at their brothers. Speaking of which, Kenny invited Russ and me to meet him at the Lake Tavern again Friday night. We're meeting at Kenny's old farm and riding together."

Ricky leaned toward me with a tweezers. I swatted him away and covered my eyebrows with my hands.

"Suit yourself. Better a unibrow than a Unabomber, I suppose. Anyway, there were some really hot guys at the Tavern last week. I think they're just summer folk—not all local people. There were some hunky college boys, even some cowboys. Oh, one guy a little older was checking me out. He says lots of things about border control, but it's all foreplay. He wants to seduce me not get my vote."

"Ricky, I'm certain you have many admirers. I thought I saw Russ checking out your ass."

"Really? He's cute and funny." Ricky picked up his hand mirror and regarded himself.

Why did I say that? "No. I just made that up. He's straighter than horse hair. At least I think he is." I turned to Ricky, took hold of his wrist, and made him look at me so he knew I was dead serious. "Don't think of guys around here as potential boyfriends."

"Jeez, Lorraine, you act like you think you're the only gay in the village. Lighten up, I bet we have lots of company, they're just not out and about."

"Yeah, well, maybe you're right, but what about what your dad said? I thought you said he'd kill you and any boyfriend you had."

"What he doesn't know won't kill me. I'm not itching to get married or anything. I would just enjoy some animated conversation if you know what I mean? You and Charity have animated conversation, don't you?" Ricky took my hand from his wrist and began filing my nails.

"No animated conversation for us lately, barely smoke signals." Suddenly maternal, I offered Ricky unsolicited advice. "Don't get the idea that because some people here know I love Charity, they accept it. I haven't exactly paved the way to anything and this isn't Hollywood or *The Ellen Show*. Minnesota and Wisconsin are the floppy breasts above the Bible belt. Hate for queers is alive and well."

"I'm just going to the Lake Tavern, having a few drinks, and talking with the men. I'm not hurting anybody." He closed the converted tackle box he used as a makeup box.

"I just think you better be careful. It might be better to seek out animated conversation in a big city." I touched his shoulder and hoped he would take my advice.

Dad walked by and did a double take. He had Allan with him. Nap time. He returned to my room after he put Allan in his bed. When he saw Ricky's makeup kit yawning on my dresser he said, "I'm next, Ricky, but only if you have pale pink polish." Dad giggled until he choked coughing. "I like you being here with Lorraine, Ricky. It's like she has a litter mate again. What mischief are you two planning?" He stood in the doorway.

"Hey, Dad. Ricky's saying Kenny invited him and Russ to the Lake Tavern again on Friday night." I said it knowing full well how concerned Dad would be.

The news suppressed both Dad's giggling and coughing. His eyebrows scrunched closer together and his eyes flashed back and forth from me to Ricky. "That's a rough crowd drinks at the Tavern." He drank in Ricky's expectant, innocent face. Dad smiled and added, "They do have a good burger with fried onions and Grain Belt on tap."

"Grandpa, are you going to read me a story?" Allan called from the bedroom he shared with Kenny.

"I'm coming," he called to Allan. Before he left, he turned to Ricky. "Don't let those boys talk you into anything, Ricky."

I heard Momma's heavy feet on the stairs. She peeked into my room. Her eyes got big when she saw Ricky in my room with me. "Oh, oh, I'll just put these clean clothes on the dresser here. Don't let me interrupt anything." She flopped my clothes down and backed out and closed the door behind her.

Ricky and I looked at each other and laughed.

"You know your momma may be happy now, but it's just going to disappoint her later when she finds out we aren't in here to make out."

"Yeah, I know, but maybe we can give her a few minutes of satisfaction."

Chapter Seven

"MARK MY WORDS, we're going to find out he did something in the city that got him exiled out in our direction." Momma dealt out paper plates to Dad, Kenny, Ricky, Allan, and me. As she served up leftover meatloaf, mashed potatoes, and peas she also offered a hearty helping of her opinion of Dr. Jacks, the doctor assigned to run Bend's first ever medical clinic. "They got rid of him and now they can say Bend has a doctor and the school can say us nursing students have a qualified professional to guide us during our clinicals. It's like people in small towns don't warrant a good doctor."

Momma completed her nursing classes just in time to begin her clinical training at the Bend Community Clinic. I suspected the main reason Momma disliked Dr. Jacks was altitude. Dr. Jacks was top dog; doctor trumped nurse. Nobody had ever trumped Momma. She burned with anger. Momma never signed onto anything unless she ran it: her marriage to Dad, parenting, and working as a waitress at Big Will's Diner all those years. She hadn't had a boss since childhood and she fired her parents as soon as she could leave home.

"Bend only got a clinic because of a federal grant. Doctor Jacks came with the package. Him and his fancy woolen suits, fancy cars and trucks. He's a show-off." Momma waved her hand at me. "Did you know he even drinks out at the tavern most nights and weekends? And he smokes. Not enough breath mints and gum in the world to cover up that stink." Momma eyed Dad for a moment. Dad lowered his head.

Even once Momma sat down, she didn't eat right away. She chewed on her thumbnail, fuming and scheming. "It's not that he's flatulent or don't wash his hands, it's just he's small-minded. He won't let me put a bowl of condoms on the counter. He said it would offend people. His ideas about medicine and public health are stuck in the '50s and so are his ideas about people."

To me a mind set in the '50s seemed like a perfect match for Momma. She was more *Father Knows Best* than HBO or Showtime, but Becky's early death and school had changed Momma some. She acted like she noticed a bit more gray than black and white. I had to admit that college made her seem like she knew more of the wider world. Maybe she did. She had at least met white people from other counties and a handful of people of color by going to school. And, as she reminded me, she saw movies and read books about the world.

"What's with the paper plates?" I asked.

If looks could kill, Momma slayed me right at the dinner table.

Dad jumped in as usual. "That's my reasoning. What with everybody working or going to school or both...it made sense to reduce some of the housework around here."

Just that quick Momma stood up and fled out the door, calling over her shoulder that she had some errands to run. I wondered if hell had frozen over. Momma permitted the use of paper plates for dinner and she served leftovers for the second time in a week.

AFTER DINNER, I pondered Momma's education and new shortcuts as I drove through town on my way to check if Charity happened to be home. Kenny had left for a movie with Ramona. Ricky had the dogs in rollers, and Dad had Allan with him on their way to the barn. Dad told me to go "air out." He'd probably tired of me moping around, calling Charity over and over and gazing out of the window like she might magically appear.

When I drove by the Bend Community Clinic, I did a double-take. Twitch's Jeep edged up alongside Momma's battered station wagon in the clinic parking lot. Odd. My heart stopped. The last time they collaborated on anything was when Becky was sick. I hoped their current confab had nothing to do with sickness, injury or death. Momma and Twitch never just got together to talk. They tolerated each other because Twitch was my dad's best friend and my biological father and mentor, but it seemed Momma wanted very little to do with him. Twitch never said anything blatantly negative to me about Momma. He acknowledged her strength and power, but he had not been conscripted as a soldier in her army.

I suppose for Momma, seeing Twitch reminded her she had had a one-night-stand with him and got pregnant with Becky and me just before she met my dad and fell in love and married him. Maybe she counted it as a mistake on her part—the mark soiling an otherwise perfect record. Maybe she thought about it every time she saw me and that's why she couldn't accept me for being lesbian, one more spot on her record. Maybe she thought about Becky being dead every time she glimpsed me and it made her sad and angry.

I had neither the heart nor constitution to ponder all those things but thinking about Momma and Twitch being alone together piqued my curiosity enough that I pulled my truck into the clinic parking lot. I parked next to a little red sports car. Then I watched Dr. Jacks remove his suit coat, lay it over the backseat of the sports car, and fold himself up to fit behind the wheel. I waved at him and he waved back, although I doubt he knew who I was. I stepped on fresh gum which stuck to my work boot and promptly picked up three cigarette filters that had been littered by where I parked.

The clinic door had been left unlocked. I entered but flipped the deadlock behind me. It was after six, closing time. Perhaps the pedestrian duties of locking the clinic didn't fall to Dr. Jacks. I passed through the empty reception area. The smell of disinfectant and watermelon room deodorizer hung in the air. The lobby furniture hadn't yet succumbed to wear and filth. The magazines on the tables were fanned out neatly and probably at least current. A better daughter would have called out to alert anyone in the clinic that I'd entered. I didn't call out. I listened. I heard Momma and Twitch arguing so obviously I had to eavesdrop until I could interrupt.

"Just what're you suggesting?" Twitch asked Momma. "She's pregnant?"

"Shush, keep your voice down. That girl's only sixteen years old, but she's built like a thirteen-year-old. She's too young to have a baby."

"Don't you think I know that? Christ."

"No need to swear, Ben." Momma always called Twitch by his given name rather than his nickname.

"Keep your religious gobbledygook to yourself, Peggy. I'll swear if I goddamn want to."

"Let's focus. What're we going to do?"

"What do you mean? You said she had a miscarriage. What can we do?"

"That's why I called you to meet me here. Maybe she had it or just started it and Dr. Jacks sent her home to finish on her own. And if she did have a miscarriage and if some nasty man got her pregnant once, he'll get her pregnant again."

"Peggy, what do you mean 'some nasty man'? Like we don't know who did it. It had to have been McGerber. Lorraine told me he's fostering her. Creep!"

Addie. Shit. I leaned back against the wall in the shadows thinking about that young, thin girl being forced into sex with McGerber.

"Did she say the holy man had sex with her, Peggy?"

"She wouldn't tell me. Not that it would do any good if she named him."

"Why? McGerber can go to jail and hell just like the rest of us."

"You fool, McGerber is a pillar of the church. She's probably not going to name him, and we can't just go accusing him of anything. Although, she does live alone with him and his wife is dead. God knows you men will have sex with anything if you feel the need."

"Yes, Peggy, I think we've already established that some of us men make damn poor decisions about who we have sex with. Not me, but some men do."

"He's a widower and old," Momma said. "Why can't he just forget about sex?"

"Not only that, McGerber has a lot of sheep," Twitch said.

"Just stop it. Let me think," Momma said. "She's not in school. She's not from here. How could she have a boyfriend? She could have met someone at church. There's farm workers to consider I suppose. I hate to think McGerber did something so awful."

"What about the sheriff?" Twitch said.

"You actually think the sheriff violated the girl?" Momma said.

"No. I mean we can tell him what we know, and he can investigate and arrest the rapist."

"You know Sheriff Scrogrum couldn't solve a crime unless he tripped on the evidence and somebody else explained what he'd found. And our new doctor, Doctor Jacks, won't help. He seemed mad at the girl for coming here. He just told me to clean up the blood and he didn't even tell the young thing what happened to her. He had the nerve to hush me when I tried to ask Addie about somebody touching her. He said, 'It's merely God cleaning house.' Then he forbade me, forbade me I tell you, from calling her placement social worker with what he called 'unfounded gossip.' The sheriff won't believe us any better. I don't trust them. They'll just put that young girl through hell while McGerber tells his side."

"Watch your language, Peggy."

When it seemed they'd hit an impasse of sorts, I gave up my position eavesdropping from the adjoining exam room and stepped out to where Momma and Twitch had been talking.

"Lorraine?" Momma said. She took up her *I am mighty pissed* pose. "What're you doing here? Is it Joseph? Are Allan and Ricky okay?"

"They're fine. I just saw both your vehicles and pulled in to talk with you." I hoped she wouldn't ask me what I wanted to talk about. I couldn't think of a thing. "Doctor Jacks must have left the door unlocked. There wasn't anybody at reception. I wasn't intending to eavesdrop... exactly."

"What'd you hear?" Twitch asked.

"Enough," I said. "Addie's body rejected the devil's spawn. McGerber is a rapist and an asshole!"

"Watch your swearing," Momma and Twitch said in unison.

"If she found the note I put in her dress pocket," Momma said, "Addie's going to be here in a little while. I told her to slip out of the potluck dinner at church study and come see me at the clinic. Poor thing."

"Did Addie come here on her own when she had the miscarriage?" I asked.

"No. That nasty man brought her here," Momma said. "He said she was having trouble with her womanly time and seemed to be bleeding pretty heavy. The fool. She was having a miscarriage. She ain't but a child herself."

Momma bit her nails like she did when she put on the big think.

"McGerber. That pious asshole. He must think he can get away with anything. What if she gets pregnant again?" I didn't think my hate for McGerber could grow any bigger, but it did.

"We've got to help her," Momma said. "She's only sixteen years old."

It surprised me to hear she'd made sixteen.

Twitch shook his head and paced. "Kids aren't made for having kids."

"So, you agree about what we have to do?" Momma asked Twitch.

Twitch eyed Momma and looked away. He said nothing, he just paced.

"What do we have to do?" I asked.

"You shouldn't even be part of this discussion," Twitch said. "You sure as hell ain't going to be a part of a birth control discussion or an abortion."

"Abortion? What're you talking about? That's not fair." My heart sank.

"If I had my way, there'd be no abortion," Twitch said. "I'd neuter McGerber!"

"We'll talk to her tonight," Momma said. "Did you bring the bananas and condoms?"

"I thought you were joking about the bananas," Twitch said. "I think I can come up with a condom."

I laughed. Both Momma and I knew Twitch probably didn't leave the house without condoms—at least not since an unexpected lesson when he got Momma pregnant with my sister Becky and me.

"It isn't that I want the girl putting a raincoat on that nasty man, but he's primed her for more trauma and early sexual experimentation. She should know about condoms. I have the better bet right here." Momma held up a plastic package with small punch-out pills I could only assume were birth control pills. I'd never actually seen them in person.

Twitch was green and sweat beaded along his brow. He stopped pacing and leaned against an exam table with his head in his hands. "I'm not made for this. I'm a vet for God's sake."

A pounding noise like a break-in echoed from the lobby of the clinic. All three of us rushed to the lobby to investigate. Twitch held a broom like a club. Momma had a metal emesis basin, and for some reason I had grabbed a stethoscope. To be of any use I would need to get close enough to strangle an intruder. We crept forward, single file, Momma in the lead at first and then Twitch hustled in front of Momma. "Jesus Christ, would you let me be the man in something?" He stepped into the waiting room. The motion detector triggered the automatic lights and florescent glare shone across the room to the glass clinic door.

No weapons were needed. It was Addie.

Momma unlocked the door and let Addie in. Addie screamed and cried as blood streaked her legs. Her once white anklets were crimson above her buckle shoes.

"Mrs. Tyler, I'm bleeding," Addie said. "I don't know what's happening. I had pads, but they can't keep up. I think my organs are falling out."

Although they had never operated together, Momma and Twitch worked like a well-rehearsed team. *I'm glad Dad isn't seeing this.* Twitch and Momma's interplay was both unsettling and awesome. They led Addie back to an exam room. Addie recognized me from our meeting at McGerber's farm and saving those kittens. She grabbed my hand and pulled me along with her.

"Vet, I'm scared. It's one thing not to obey him about the kittens, but this?"

"It's going to be okay," I said. "Call me Lorraine. I'll stay right here with you."

Momma and Twitch helped Addie up onto a paper-covered exam table. I held Addie's hand while Momma and Twitch whispered together in the hallway. Twitch came back in the room and winked at Addie.

"Addie, Mrs. Tyler and I are going to get that bleeding to stop."

Addie cried and her legs moved with agitation.

I petted her hand and cooed that she was going to be all right. I didn't know how convincing I sounded. I didn't know if I believed myself. Staying calm is a lot easier when the patient has fur or hooves. This people emergency stuff was stressful.

"Everything's going to be okay, Addie. You're going to be fine. You are in good hands." I knew at least the last part was true.

Momma slipped Addie's shoes off. "Addie, I need you to slip your panties off. Can you lift your hips for me? That's right, dear. I'll get you something else to wear before you go out and I'll get these clothes washed up for you."

Addie lay nude from the waist down, partially covered in a blanket, and her feet were in those damn exam table stirrups which were only a little less creepy when Momma covered them with pink socks. Momma and Twitch had put on gowns, gloves, and masks, and Momma opened a prepackaged tray of sterile instruments and another bundle of packing.

The volume of blood and pulpy masses left little doubt that she'd miscarried. I'd seen it a couple of times before, but only in animals. Once, when a pregnant sheep aborted after being chased by dogs and once when a cow expelled her calf early because of a bacterial disease. The miscarriage that began with cramping and bleeding earlier in the day finished off now. No abortion necessary. Addie's body had expelled the baby before it had time to grow to something bigger, doing the job without help from anybody.

"Honey, you're going to be just fine," Momma told Addie. "You had a miscarriage. Did you know you were pregnant, Addie?"

"No," Addie said. "I can't be. You can't get pregnant the first time."

Momma, Twitch, and I exchanged looks. Addie had plenty of company with people who held that mistaken notion.

"The first time and every time counts," Momma said. Of course, she knew this from her own experience too. She glanced at Twitch and back to Addie. "Some people even get pregnant although they're using birth control."

"Oh," Addie said. She appeared sheepish like she'd been caught in an awfully foolish mistake.

"The baby is gone, honey. Your body said it wasn't ready to have a baby yet." Tears stained Momma's mask.

"Did I do something wrong that the baby died?" Addie asked. "Will I be able to have babies later?"

"No and yes. No, you didn't do anything wrong and yes, you can have babies later after college and graduate school. For now, your body's just not ready." Momma still wore bloody gloves, but I watched Momma's face. Her eyes caressed Addie every bit as much as Momma would've if her hands were clean.

Twitch had a syringe and a specimen jar and put some expelled tissue in the jar. Addie watched him.

"Do you want me to take that and keep it or is it for...him?"

"No, Addie. I want to keep this. This is proof of who did this to you. It will help us stop him from doing this again." Twitch capped the jar and took off his mask and gloves.

"I don't want to get anybody in trouble," Addie said. "He's not at the farm."

"Lorraine, there're some scrubs in the cabinet in the next room. Get Addie a pair that might fit her—the prettiest pair you can find." Then Momma took off her gloves and mask and stroked Addie's face with her big hand. "Who did this, honey?"

Momma shooed me out, but of course I listened from the hall. I could hear everything, but only see Twitch from where I stood.

"Who had sex with you?" Momma asked.

"I'm not saying." Addie ran her fingers over her mouth like she zipped her lips.

I returned and when I bent closer to cover her shoulders with a blanket, she whispered, "The old fart will be so mad at me."

Both Momma and Twitch must have heard her and reached the same conclusion I did.

Twitch's jaw tightened.

Momma stepped in front of him. "Honey, you don't have to worry about Mister McGerber. I'm going to take you home to my house and feed you until you have some meat on your bones."

"Can I really come to your house?" Addie asked.

The house is filling up.

Momma nodded.

I held some pale pink scrubs with pictures of rabbits playing various musical instruments on the top and plain pink drawstring bottoms.

Twitch had taken Addie's hand. "I'll deal with McGerber." Then Twitch turned to Momma. "Peggy, initial and date this jar, would you?" He handed her the jar with some tissue in it from the miscarriage.

Momma initialed and dated the label on the bottle.

"I don't think you can prove anything with that and if you can, it would be a costly test in some big city laboratory," I said.

"McGerber won't know that." Twitch winked at me. "I'm going to put this in a safe place for insurance and then I'm going to church."

"Can I come?" I asked. *Wow, mark this day on the calendar. I asked to go to church.* Going to church had never exactly excited me unless Charity was going to be there. Twitch wasn't an avid worshipper either, but he'd go to the church to find and confront McGerber. As Twitch surely knew, I'd have liked nothing better than to see McGerber squirm for a change. Maybe Twitch was trying to make up for sending me to the old man's farm weeks prior. He scrutinized Momma briefly. She didn't say anything. Then Twitch waved for me to follow him.

"Momma, can you get Addie to our house by yourself?"

"Of course, I can. I'm putting her in your room, so she doesn't have to do any stairs," Momma said. "You sleep upstairs with Allan, Kenny, and Ricky for now. No messing around up there!"

Like me messing with them or any man was a remote possibility.

Chapter Eight

TWITCH USED ABOUT every swear I'd ever heard and two or three I'd never heard before as he drove the couple of blocks to the church where McGerber worshiped. The church had fewer and smaller stained-glass windows than the Catholic church. Arborvitae shrubs, passing as landscaping, lined the perimeter of the building and sidewalks. Our family attended that church too—Momma under the force of her religious convictions, Dad and I under the force of Momma. Lately, not even Momma could make me go since Charity wasn't home to go with me, and I was still trying to make sense of Becky killing herself thinking God required her sacrifice. I doubted Twitch had ever been there before other than for funerals or weddings—Becky's had been held there.

The monthly potluck dinner had ended. My stomach ached a bit. I could almost taste the goulash and seven-layer bars. Thinking of it made me miss church a little. I lowered my head and avoided eye contact. Kind people, generous good-hearted people I'd known all my life had brought their hot dishes, Jell-O salads, chips, and bars to the church. The food, plates, silverware, and lemonade thermos and fifty-cup coffee urn covered most of two banquet tables. A white canopy sheltered five or six banquet tables and an army of khaki folding chairs. As the men milled around, women and high school age kids cleared the tables, bringing the leftovers and dishes through the church's side door and down the basement into the kitchen.

If the schedule hadn't changed I knew there'd be an evening Bible study after the meal. I remembered the few times I'd gone and had my fill of comfort food and fought sleep as I sat through the Bible lesson. That night a handful of believers scurried out of the brown brick edifice and down the concrete stairs to the parking lot. They were gutsy enough to attend the meal, but skipped out on the Bible study.

Pastor Grind stood solid like a gargoyle at the top of the cement steps watching and probably judging everything. McGerber joined Grind. The holy duo gassed with each other and observed the estate. McGerber probably evaluated the youth and got excited thinking about awarding his scholarship the next spring. Maybe he searched for Addie. The youth who weren't assisting with clean-up stood talking on the church steps.

Twitch got out of the Jeep. "Come on!" I followed.

"McGerber!" Twitch called him before he'd finished with Pastor Grind. "McGerber, come down off the mountain top."

McGerber mumbled something to Pastor Grind and descended the steps. He probably wondered if Twitch came to hit him again.

"What do you want?" McGerber sneered. Pastor Grind followed on McGerber's heels. I saw some of Charity's features in Grind's face. He didn't have her perfect nose, but his eyes, he had the same hound-dog-brown eyes as Charity. I hoped he could look on me with some compassion.

Twitch raised his head. "Thought you might want to know. Addie won't be home tonight or ever if I can help it."

"Addie?" McGerber said. He tilted his head and looked befuddled. "What have you done with...?"

"Stay away from her. You sick bastard!" Twitch said. "She came to the clinic."

"I know that. I brought her to the clinic, but she's not sick." McGerber babbled red-faced. "Her womanly..."

"No, she's not sick and she ain't pregnant anymore either," Twitch shouted.

I didn't like that he'd said the P-word so loud with so many people still around. I could almost feel the rush of air as people's heads turned to listen in on this private conversation. What if Addie had to go to Bend High School in the fall? These kids would tell what they'd heard just as certain as anyone else would. She'd be gossiped about every day and harassed by boys who thought it made her a whore. They'd bully her and about every one of them would wish for a chance to have sex with her too.

"Pregnant? How could that girl..."

"Like you don't know," Twitch said.

"What?" McGerber wobbled and took a step back. Finally, Twitch's implication seemed to on him. He staggered backwards, more stricken than the day Twitch hit him in the face. I felt a little sorry for him.

"I've got the tissue sample to prove it." Twitch patted his coat pocket. "If you don't want to be some prison inmate's girlfriend you better stay away from her." Then Twitch yelled at Pastor Grind. "Hey, Padre, you're keeping some pretty poor company. Did you have any part in that girl being put in foster care with this pervert?"

"Gentlemen, let's go into my office," Pastor Grind said. "Don't air such serious allegations and Addie's private business out here like this."

I thought it was one of the wisest things I'd ever heard come out of Grind's mouth, but no way in hell did I ever want to be in his office again. Neither McGerber nor Twitch seemed interested in having a visit in Pastor Grind's office either.

McGerber's face shone purple in the fading evening light and I thought he might stroke out. "You'll pay for these lies, Twitchell. All of the ungodly will pay." He flashed an evil eye at me and then glared at Twitch. "You're nothing but a drunken letch."

"You know, McGerber, you're right. I'm a drunk and I've even had affairs with married women. Shame on me for all I've done. God, if there is a God, might just send me straight to hell for the things I've done, if there is a hell. But God damn it, shame on you for being the hypocrite you are and damn you for being sexual with a child."

McGerber threw a punch at Twitch that might have landed if Pastor Grind hadn't grabbed the old man from behind.

"There'll be no violence here, gentlemen." Pastor Grind locked his arms around McGerber's torso and pinned him. It would have been a good time to slug them both, but Twitch didn't raise his fists.

The old man struggled against Grind's hold but couldn't break loose. Charity's dad was a tall, muscular guy when it came down to it. He easily controlled McGerber without breaking a sweat or losing his balance.

"Now, Julian Carver McGerber, calm yourself down," Pastor Grind said. "I'm strong enough and stubborn enough to restrain you for several hours if that's what it takes to keep you from making a fool of yourself."

"You let me go, Allister," McGerber said, but he quit fighting against Grind. Once Grind released him

McGerber straightened his suit coat, but he slumped as he turned to face Grind. Maybe he felt the weight of what he'd done. At least he felt the weight of the accusation.

"You can't possibly believe I would lay with that girl?" McGerber whimpered to Grind. "I would never defile a child or the memory of my Mary." Then McGerber turned to Twitch and me.

"This isn't over, Twitchell." McGerber said. He straightened his suit again, ran his fingers over his mostly bald head and subdued the remaining gray hair around his ears. Then he walked to his car, got in, and drove away.

"Are you certain about what you said?" Grind regarded Twitch and me. "I've never seen anything in him that would make me suspect such a thing."

"Addie, the girl, she's been living with McGerber," Twitch said. "I saw the miscarriage myself. She was pregnant and miscarried, and I heard her say she's afraid McGerber's going to be mad at her about it. Sounds pretty clear to me."

"Where's Addie?" Grind asked. "Do you need anything from me? I will help in any way I can. She certainly requires my counsel."

Yeah right, he'd probably lecture her about disappointing God by having premarital sex.

"Thanks, Padre, but the rest of us sinners have got it covered. The girl miscarried tonight at the clinic. She's out at the Tyler place. Peggy's attending to her."

"I'll call the County social worker who arranged the placement first thing in the morning," Grind said.

I had to ask him. "You won't try to take her back to him, will you?"

"No, Lorraine. I won't do that. It'll be up to social services. I won't interfere."

I wished I could believe him. I wished he could understand and accept that I loved his daughter. *There's nothing to fear from love.*

Chapter Nine

TWITCH DROPPED ME back at my truck. He said he wanted to get the specimen over to his office and make some notes about the night's events. I drove home by way of Charity's house. No truck in the yard. No lights in the studio apartment above the garage. Less hope in my heart. When I got home, I found Dad seated at the kitchen table. The dogs, Pants, Sniff, and Satan, slept at his feet, rousing only to see if I was someone they should bark at, lick, or bite. They flopped back onto the floor under the table, groaned, stretched, and went back to sleep. Dad nursed a bottle of beer. He played solitaire with a battered deck of playing cards with pictures of fish on them. I moved one of his black jacks to a red queen before either of us spoke.

He weakly slapped at my hand. "I thought you'd be at Charity's tonight?"

"You and me both. I stopped there, but..." I shook my head and shrugged. "I think she's been abducted by aliens, or maybe the Rapture. I can't find her anywhere. Ricky home? I saw his car."

"Yep, he went to bed early. He said he needed his beauty rest." Dad smiled and shook his head. "There's some big doings at the Tavern this weekend."

"Momma or Twitch call you? You hear what happened?"

"Yep." He finished his bottle of beer.

Dad drinking in the house, these are strange times. He usually had his beer by himself in the barn because every time he brought any in the house, Momma hid it. "Where did you find it this time?'

"It was in the clothes hamper. It isn't cold, but some days require beer even if it's warm."

"Addie in my room?"

"Yep."

"You're sure quiet. I thought for certain tonight's fiasco would warrant an animal story to explain the complex mistakes of the human animal." My dad always had an animal story to explain something or teach some important lesson.

"I don't know what to think. I just don't see McGerber as a man who'd molest a child." Dad gathered his playing cards into a messy pile.

"I wouldn't put anything past McGerber. He acts so self-righteous in front of people, but I think he's evil."

"He's self-righteous, but he's also a scared kind of man. He couldn't take the shame of being caught at something like this and there's no way he wouldn't get caught. He wasn't keeping that girl hidden. It don't make sense to me." He shrugged. "Maybe she has a boyfriend."

I noodled on the thought a full four seconds before dismissing the idea.

Dad slapped the deck of cards on the table and began unlacing his boots. Once he'd pulled them off he massaged his feet through his gray tube socks. My dad didn't say anything important without thinking about his words. He believed a person should think before they speak and read before they think.

I tried to catch him, make him show his true heart. "What do you think of abortion?" I asked.

"Christ, abortion, that's a big kettle of fish. Ask me something easier."

"Nope, this is just the sort of thing a daughter should ask her dad. Babies aren't just women's business."

He sighted me in. "I don't like the idea of abortion at all. I wish there'd never in this world be another child conceived who's not wanted." He removed his socks and put his bare feet on the kitchen linoleum and wiggled his toes and flexed his arches. "Children should be safe and brought into a home that can provide at least a decent effort at parenting."

"It seems like you were leading up to a big 'but' in your wishes, Dad."

"Well, you asked me if I had an animal story. I guess I do. Every kind of animal has miscarriages, which as you know as a vet, are spontaneous abortions. Nature takes care of some potential problems without ever consulting the church, the government, or social media. And, all kinds of animals—fish, birds, insects, amphibians, and even mammals—kill their young. It's a sore subject when it comes to the human animal. We wouldn't have any debate if a baby curled its little fingers around our thumb. If somebody killed that baby we would've reached a pretty quick consensus that it was murder, insanity at the least. But when the baby is still growing inside a woman's body, it gets murky. And if the baby came to be because of rape or incest, then there're some other questions for some people." He examined his feet.

"I don't like the idea of abortion either, I guess," I said. "I don't know how I'd feel if it was my body or my daughter's body. I don't think I'd like people like McGerber deciding whether I had a baby or not. I definitely hate that there are people who will rape women and children and then call them whores and condemn them for wanting an abortion."

"I can never honestly say I know what it is like for a woman," Dad said. "I don't much fear being raped or ever being pregnant. All I can hang on to is that I think I have love for every child that could be born, and I wouldn't wish anyone to have to make the decision not to have a baby or not to keep it." He stood up. "Your momma would tell you if I'd had my way, we'd have had a dozen babies around here." He grinned. "I like the house filling up. Maybe I should quit the lumber business and open an orphanage or home for young mothers? None of those young lives—mommas or babies—have to go to waste. And if you asked me I'd tell you the greatest skill a man can learn is to tenderly raise a child."

He walked toward his and Momma's bedroom but stopped in the doorway. "You know, there's plenty of men who would spend a lot more time at home if they dared take a true taste of what it's like to care for a child and have them love them back. I'm sure as hell glad I didn't miss being a dad—hard job, but the best job I ever had." He went in the bedroom and closed the door.

Movement from the darkness of the living room startled me. Momma'd been sitting by herself in the dark, probably adding a few of my sins to her notebook. She joined me at the kitchen table.

"It's legal you know?" Momma said.

"Yeah, I know. I just didn't imagine you'd be for it."

"Not being against it being legal isn't the same as being for it. It just doesn't make it go away by calling it against the law. I've seen some of the pictures and read the stories about the botched abortions and babies put in the trash because a young girl felt abandoned or was let down by all the other people with a horse in the race, like her parents and child's father and his parents. What if Becky had hidden or ended her pregnancy because she worried nobody would help her? I can't imagine not having that little one in this world. Promise me, Lorraine, don't ever hide your being pregnant or kill it. I'm like your dad. I wish there'd never have to be another one, but I think it is important that women make the decision with their doctor and other people who truly love her."

"Would you have talked to Addie about having an abortion if she didn't already miscarry?"

"I don't know. I thought I would. Now, I don't have to know."

"Would you've done the abortion?"

"Are those my only choices? If it was between that and having a young girl dealing with becoming a mother through rape by an old man..." She stopped talking for a few beats. "I'm glad I don't have to know what I'd have done. Doctor Jacks, my boss, would never do it. He would blame Addie for getting herself that way." She scratched something in her notebook, slammed it shut, got up from the table, and poured herself a glass of milk.

I went upstairs to bed.

Chapter Ten

THE NEXT MORNING, Mom, Dad, and Kenny went to their respective jobs, and I stayed home with Ricky, Addie, and Allan. Allan. Allan. *It's better than calling him Kenny Jr.,* I said a few times as I kissed his sweet cheeks. Kenny had tucked him in with me before he went off to work. He grinned broadly, squirmed, and fake snored even though for the past half hour he'd been poking me and pulling my eyelids up asking if I was awake. I took him downstairs to the kitchen. He got up on a kitchen chair and began lining up his plastic animals. The phone rang before 9:00 a.m. Pastor Grind. Nothing good had ever come from a phone call from Grind.

"Lorraine, Reverend Grind here. I wanted to tell your mother that the same County social worker who placed Addie at McGerber's house will be coming to your house this morning to pick up Addie and take her to a new placement."

"Momma's at the clinic. Dad's at the lumber yard. Christ, just what I need—some bureaucratic-do-gooder with more questions than sense and too much time on her hands," I said to Grind over the phone.

"Lorraine, could you try to have an open mind and try not to use the Lord's name in vain? This worker was just doing her job. I doubt she intended for Addie to get pregnant and miscarry."

"Yeah, I suppose you're right." I hung up the phone and surveyed the house.

A few minutes later Addie awakened and joined Allan and me in the kitchen. Ricky entered a few seconds behind Addie. Ricky and Addie were meeting for the first time as far as I knew, but Ricky fawned on her like they were long-lost litter mates. He brushed Addie's hair and prattled on about her perfect skin. Addie ate up Ricky's attention like she'd been starving for it.

All I have to offer you is my old room and cereal for breakfast.

"Do you really think I'm pretty?" Addie peered at herself in Ricky's hand mirror.

"You are stunning." Ricky fiddled with his color wheel and told Addie which shades of eye shadow were best for her.

"Allan and I are playing Antarctica today after breakfast." I placed a box of Cheerios on the table. "Well, Allan has already started actually." The kitchen table glistened with whipped cream, coconut flakes, powdered sugar, and melting ice cubes as Allan tramped plastic polar bears, penguins, and seals across the arctic tundra. The day before Allan and I had glued an igloo together with flour, water, and sugar cubes. I pushed the igloo to the side and made room for some cereal bowls and the carton of milk.

Addie rested her chin on her hand and stared at Ricky like she wanted to kiss him or eat him.

"I have some plans today too." I had planned on writing a letter to Charity while Allan busied himself hunting seals with polar bears. I planned to ask Charity if our relationship had died while I wasn't paying attention and if so, could it possibly be resuscitated?

Ricky and Addie ignored me. They giggled together as they over-sugared their cereal and Ricky tested lipsticks on the back of his hand.

"I should be writing to the vet school."

"I thought you were already a vet." Addie held Ricky's hand with the lipstick samples up to her face as if that accomplished anything.

"No, not yet. I got another letter from the school. They received my most recent transcript of college credits, but my spot would be forfeited if I don't confirm my enrollment date in the next ninety days."

I was emotionally wrecked, but Addie and Ricky didn't seem too interested. While they diddled with makeup and moisturizer and Allan played with his animals, I worked on a letter to Charity. Wads of failed white paper littered the floor like snowballs. Allan had sticky but edible fake snow and ice all over his hands, arms, face, and part of his head.

"Oh crap, I forgot to tell you, Addie. Your social worker is coming this morning."

I doubted official County folk abided messes very well, so I abandoned the letter I couldn't seem to write and began cleaning the kitchen. The sound of a car pulling into the yard jolted Addie off her chair.

"Marin is here. I better get my stuff. Thank you, Ricky. I hope I see you again some time." Addie kissed Ricky quickly on the cheek and bounded back to the bedroom where she'd slept the night before.

I performed my reconnaissance through the kitchen window. A bright red Toyota truck, clean and undented, was parked next to my piece of crap rusted, battered, filthy truck. The dogs, Pants, Sniff, and Satan, barked and jumped at the window and door. Pants had green rollers along his sides, and both Sniff and Satan sported pink rollers and hair nets. Ricky had gotten to them earlier in the morning. No wonder they didn't come out until a car approached. I hushed the dogs and opened the door for the social worker.

I'd never met a County social worker before, but I was prepared to hate her or at least make it clear I she'd pissed me off. How could she have placed that young girl with McGerber? How unfit did a mother have to be for her child to be better off at his house? I was ready to give the social worker one of the few pieces of my mind I had left. Damn it, my other parts were reacting strongly to seeing this woman.

I expected someone matronly, dressed in monochromatic shades of vomit and smelling like Lysol, part prison guard and part janitor, but *she's a cowgirl.* She showed me an identification badge with her picture—not half as pretty as the real thing—and the emblem for Jewitt County Human Services. The dogs sniffed at her and dropped to the floor, presenting their bellies for rubbing despite the curlers in their fur. She didn't get to them right away.

"I'm Marin England from Child Protective Services. I'm here to see Addie. Are you Miss Tyler?" she asked as she put out her hand to me.

"God, no! I'm Lorraine Tyler—the daughter. Momma's at work at the clinic." I shook her hand. It was a soft, warm hand; the pads of her fingers were pillowy. I detected no scent of Lysol, but perhaps the faint hint of lavender. I was still holding her hand when Ricky materialized in the kitchen and made a fuss about Marin's hair and skin tones, breaking the moment I shouldn't have been having. Marin listened to Ricky's patter as she scratched the dogs' undercarriage and told them what good boys they were. Ricky acted like Marin was speaking to him.

Momma would have described Marin as a big-boned gal—not fat, but tall and sturdy. I suspected she could pick me up and carry me some place. I blushed. *Why'd I think that? I shouldn't be thinking that.* She couldn't be much older than me.

Ms. England wore black cowboy boots with aqua accents in the tooled leather, black jeans, a black shirt with white pearl snaps. No cowboy hat on that French braided cascade of chestnut hair, but I would've bet good money one sat on the seat in her truck. I couldn't tell if she had tanned from outside work or was naturally bronzed.

"Please have a seat, Miss England," I said. "Could I get you some coffee?" I hoped she'd politely say no because I hadn't made any coffee.

Ricky butted in between the social worker and me. "Maybe some time you and Lorraine should go out for a real drink, maybe at the Lake Tavern. It's a local hot spot, do you know it?"

I punched Ricky's arm. "What're you doing? Get out of here. Don't you have some dogs to manicure, pedicure, or marinate?"

He appeared wounded, but at least he gathered the dogs and left the kitchen.

"Ricky is studying cosmetology," I said.

"Is he your husband?" Marin asked.

"Ricky? God no. He just lives with us, Momma found him, and he followed her home. He's my new best friend, but he'll never be anyone's husband." I offered Ms. England a cup of coffee again.

"Thank you. Call me Marin. I'm too young to be Ms. anything. I'll skip the coffee—I never learned to like the taste of it." She put her black canvas bag on a chair and inspected the kitchen. Then she gravitated to Allan. He stood on a kitchen chair where I had stationed him, washing pretend snow off his polar bears and seals.

"And who are you?" she asked him.

Allan splashed and jabbered his name, but Marin didn't catch it.

"Are you raising this fine young man? Is this your son?"

"Yes, I mean, no. Well, I'm raising Little Man, I mean Allan, but I'm not his mom. His mom, my sister, Becky, died. Now, Allan and his daddy live with us—that is with me and my parents and Ricky too."

"Sounds like this farm is the place to go if you need sanctuary," Marin said.

"It's more of a sanitarium," I said.

Marin laughed and took a pad of paper and pen from her bag. "What can you tell me about this situation with Addie? She's here, right?"

"Yeah, she's grabbing her things from my room." I waved my hand in the direction of the bedroom. "I'm not in that room too. I'm upstairs with Ricky, Kenny, and Allan. Not in the same room or anything." *God, stop your babbling and overexplaining What's wrong with you?*

"How did you meet Addie?"

"Drenching McGerber's sheep. I'm almost a vet." I stood a little taller. Then I remembered I planned to dislike the social worker. In a more serious voice, I said, "As you know, Addie is being fostered by McGerber because her momma... I really don't know what her momma did."

"I think there are a lot of similarities in values and passions between women who choose to be social workers and veterinarians." Marin tapped her pen against her chin as she looked over at me. "Don't you think?"

Marin had incredibly full lips. I lost my train of thought. The word "passions" pulsed in my brain. "To be honest, I've never compared or contrasted social workers and veterinarians, but I'll make a plan to give it some thought." I smiled like a fool.

"Did Addie tell you anything about the way Mister McGerber treated her?"

I shook the cobwebs and tendrils of lust out of my head.

"Let's see. She called him a smelly old fart, or maybe I called him that first. I'm not sure. I know he asked her to drown a litter of kittens. Then, I learned from Momma and Twitch that McGerber got her pregnant. Twitch is Doctor Twitchell, he's our local veterinarian."

Marin jotted something down on her note pad. "I talked to Doctor Twitchell at his office before I came out here. I'll ask you what I asked him." Marin separated the words of her question like she addressed an imbecile. "Did Addie say to you that Mister McGerber had sexual relations with her?"

I thought about the question and tried to remember that day at the clinic. "No, but who else could've done it? She lived with him and—"

Jot, jot, scribble, jot. Marin cut me off.

"I just need to know specific details," she said and kind of smiled and winked. "Did you hear directly from Addie that Mister McGerber touched her sexually?"

Uh oh, another person on McGerber's side. "No."
More jotting.

"Lorraine, did you ever witness any sort of inappropriate touching by Mister McGerber?"

"No." All the good feelings I had about her cowgirl outfit went right down the toilet. This felt like an interrogation designed to exonerate McGerber. I couldn't possibly like Marin if she grilled me and defended McGerber. I wanted to read what she wrote. All the writing made me think of Momma and her notebook. *This can't be good.*

"I didn't see it and Addie didn't tell me specifically that McGerber was sexual with her. Momma said McGerber brought Addie to the clinic for a heavy period and she had a miscarriage. It just seemed obvious that it must've been McGerber. You don't know him, but he's pure evil."

"Actually, I do know him." Marin wrinkled her nose like she knew she was delivering more bad news and she was right. It stunk. She said, "He and his wife have fostered children for short periods before. His references are good. I know he's religiously conservative, but there've never been any allegations of this kind or any kind against Mister McGerber."

I hoped the woman's boots were tight.

"This morning I visited your momma at the clinic and caught her before she started her morning shift," Marin said. "She told me she didn't ask Addie specifically if McGerber touched her and Addie didn't volunteer any information. I need to ask Addie what happened. I won't do it here. I'll bring Addie back to my office and interview her there, so I can put the interview on tape."

"Well, don't assume he's perfect just because he goes to church."

"I won't assume that, but I also can't assume he molested a minor without some proof. Besides, as you probably know, at sixteen, it isn't illegal for Addie to have consensual sex."

"With her foster parent? With someone older than dirt?"

"No, having sex with a foster parent would be criminal for the foster parent. Having sex with someone older, if it is consensual—you know, informed consent and not coerced or an abuse of authority—is not necessarily prosecuted as statutory rape. It's complicated."

"That's dumb. Can a sixteen-year-old give informed consent?"

"You don't have to answer, Lorraine, but how old were you when you first had sex? Was the man or woman older?"

I bit my lip. I wanted to tell her I was over eighteen when I first had sex, but my brain froze. She mentioned the possibility I'd had sex with another woman.

"Addie may have a boyfriend." She handed me a business card and a shiny brochure about a Girl's Ranch. "Addie will be staying at this ranch for the time being. You can visit her if she puts your name on a visitors' list. I'm headed there after I interview Addie at my office."

"Will Addie be safe at this ranch?"

"Yeah, the people and horses are safe for Addie. She will get a good rest and time with some amazing animals. You might like it yourself. I could take you riding. You could bring your nephew too."

Maybe I imagined it, but it seemed like Marin blushed when she asked me to visit the ranch. Or just maybe, the heat came from my own cheeks. I felt like my body had betrayed me in responding to this McGerber-defending cowgirl. Just then Addie came in the kitchen.

"Hey, Marin. Am I staying here or going with you?"

"We need to have a talk at the office and then I think it's time to go to that horse ranch I told you about when we first met. There's an immediate opening and I think you'll really like it there."

"I know I'll like the animals better than most people I've met," Addie said. "It's fine being here too. My baby died. It wasn't very big I guess. My body wasn't ready."

My heart sunk at how casually she said the words, like Allan repeating that Becky died. So young for such reality. Addie wore her own clothes again. Momma had washed and pressed them. She carried the pink scrubs she had been given at the clinic and offered them to me.

"You can keep them, if you want. They'd make good pajamas," I said. It seemed a small consolation. "The clinic won't miss them."

"Goodbye, Lorraine. I hope I get that kitten sometime." She hugged me quick and stood next to Marin.

The kitten. The sweet girl had just lost her first baby, but she called in her marker for the promise of a kitten. I swallowed hard.

"Thanks for being a good friend to Addie, Lorraine. I hope I see you again." She seemed to mean it. Marin put her pad and pen in her bag and slung the bag over her shoulder.

"I'll need to talk with you again. I mean, our family will want to know what happens—you know, with Addie."

"I won't be able to disclose information about a case to anyone without a release. Other topics of discussion are, of course, legal and welcome." Marin looked from me to Addie. "But you could visit Addie at the ranch if it is okay with Addie, and maybe she would tell you what you want to know."

Addie stepped forward. Right then, she didn't seem the timid girl I first saw in the barn.

"I'll tell you what you want to know right now, and you can still come to the ranch anytime you want. I didn't have sex with that old fart McGerber if that's what you're all thinking, but I'm not saying anything else. Tell Ricky goodbye again from me." She turned and walked out the door.

Marin raised her eyebrows and smiled at me before she followed Addie to the truck.

Crap. I knew I shouldn't be disappointed that McGerber wasn't a child molester, but for some reason I felt let down. At least Marin didn't say "I told you so" before she left.

I turned my attention to Allan. He'd washed and rinsed his plastic animals. I came up behind him and planted raspberries on his neck below his blond hair. He giggled and squirmed but persisted in his task. He lined up his animals on the kitchen table by type and loyalty— first came the polar bears, then the seals, and penguins. I picked up one of his penguins as I considered attempting another letter to Charity, but before I got even a word on paper, Ricky buzzed back in the kitchen like a pestering mosquito. He stood close to me.

"So? Did you ask her out? Don't tell me, she asked you to a rodeo?"

"What're you talking about? You goof!"

"Rodeo, you doowf," Allan mimicked.

Ricky lowered his head and leered at me through his dark eyelashes. "You had to know that girl likes girls. Are you telling me you didn't notice?"

"How do you know? What makes you an expert on recognizing lesbians?"

"It's a gift. Whenever I meet a lesbian I either want to tell her all my secrets or repair her wardrobe, makeup, and hair."

"Which thing did you want to work on when you saw me?" I regretted the question as soon as it left my mouth because of course he told me.

"Everything." Ricky rolled his big brown eyes. "No offense, Lorraine, but you've a lot of work areas. Don't get me wrong, you're pretty in that wholesome farm girl way, but you dress like a scarecrow, your hair always looks like you live in a wind tunnel, and you waste your beautiful eyes and high cheekbones by forbidding them to know makeup and people get distracted wondering what happened to your hair."

"Wow, at least you didn't mean to offend me."

"I can help you if you want to do some fixing up for a date with Marin."

"Why would I date Marin? I have a girlfriend, Charity."

"You keep saying that, but I've lived with you and your folks for weeks now and I think I have glimpsed her only once." Ricky put the polar bears in compromising positions with the seals. "I'm beginning to wonder if she's really your girlfriend."

"She's still my girlfriend." *I hoped.* "At least she's not some photograph that comes with a new wallet." I regretted the statement but didn't stop myself.

"She's a girlfriend," Allan said.

"I'm sorry I said that, Ricky. Charity is a sensitive topic and well, I did notice Marin, but I felt kind of wicked about it."

"It's not wicked, it's natural. Did I hear her invite you to a ranch to ride horses?" His eyes got big.

"Yeah, so?" I knew what he meant, but I refused to divulge my plans.

Ricky disengaged the polar bears and seals, stood up, and whispered into my ear, "Horse riding is incredible foreplay, or so I have been told." He wiggled his little butt as he left the room which made me wonder if he had ridden some horses himself.

I thought I would wet my pants laughing.

"What do you think, Allan? Would you like to see some real horses?"

"Yes."

Maybe God or the universe talks to queers too. Was He saying, "Get ye to a ranch for girls?" And if God says that to a queer girl, what's she supposed to do?

Chapter Eleven

A COUPLE OF weeks passed. If what happened wouldn't have happened, would I have called Marin and asked to go horseback riding? Would I have finished the letter I started to Charity a hundred times? I will never know because again nothing made sense in the sleepy town of Bend anymore. My whole world changed again with just a phone call.

One o'clock in the morning the phone rings. Dad got there first. If it had been a normal time of day, he wouldn't have answered the contraption. He hated the phone, but his good sense told him only extraordinary news came if the phone rang between the hours of midnight and six in the morning.

"Who's calling? God damn it. What are you talking about?" Dad yelled into the phone.

"Who was that?" I asked Dad after he hung up the phone.

He struggled with pulling on his boots and totally missed the fact he hadn't yet put on his pants. He stood in the kitchen in undershorts and a dingy T-shirt. The dogs jumped at his feet, caught up in the panic. "I don't know. I guess I just had what you'd call an anonymous tip. Somebody—sounded like a man—said Ricky needs help some place by the County line. I'll go check on Ricky. You stay here."

Like that's going to happen.

Dad said he didn't want to wake Momma. I told him I would scream for her right that minute unless he'd let me go with him to find Ricky. Dad remedied his wardrobe—put on his standard blue chambray work shirt, dark green Dickey work pants, tube socks, and Red Wing boots. I got dressed too. We took Dad's truck and searched for Ricky.

The County line skirted the opposite side of our farm, Kenny's folks' old farm and Gerry Narrow's land. Gerry had been the one who harbored Becky and first told us that Becky was sick. It wasn't at all far as the crow flies, but it measured a few miles if you needed to drive to catch it. The moon was plump in the sky. Dad weaved the truck down the road searching on both sides for signs of Ricky. Dad's headlights reflected off the eyes of raccoons in the ditches and deer in the fields. Trees swayed in the wind that had come up since dark. Over the hill past the Czech place we came upon an approach. Ricky's car, a silver well-used Honda Civic, was parked there. Everything went into muted slow motion.

The red taillights of Ricky's car reflected off the gravel. The lighting made the world blurry and obscure, like how I imagined a movie set during a nighttime shoot. Once we pulled up flush to Ricky's car it was clear if this country view was a movie shoot, it was a horror film. The engine wasn't running, but the car doors were open. The dome light illuminated what appeared to be an empty car. The headlights splashed light on a wooden gate where someone stood awkwardly.

Dad parked on the roadside behind Ricky's car. He put on his flashers and left the headlights on. I got out of the truck and tried to make sense of the scene.

My eyes adjusted. Ricky. He wasn't standing. He hung there, strapped to the fence with rope or cord. He resembled the gory picture of Jesus in the Sunday school room at church.

His good white shirt with the little stand-up collar was torn and bloodstained. There was so much blood on his shirt and down his legs that I worried he couldn't have had any left in him. *Where are his pants? Where is his other shoe?*

Blood obscured his face. His chocolate, almond-shaped eyes were hidden under darkening, swollen lids, his perfect nose—smashed flat, his mouth hung open, his lips torn, his teeth were pink with blood and maybe some were chipped or missing. I couldn't tell. His head fell to the side and his chin rested on his collarbone. *He's broken. Oh God, don't let him die too!*

"Ricky, Ricky, Ricky!" I couldn't stop saying his name. Maybe it could hold him to earth. I took his head in my hands and then tried to hold his body up. His head fell to my shoulder. His hair was slick with blood. His breath was shallow and raspy. Dad cut him loose from the fence. He dropped into my arms, heavier than his actual mass because of the burden put on him. Dad and I wrapped him in a blanket from the truck. Dad carried him to the truck. I didn't bother to search for his missing shoes and pants. I only wanted him—like he belonged to our family and I had to get him away from whatever else might be lurking to get him.

"Ricky, Ricky, I am so sorry," I cried.

I didn't know how long he'd been strapped to that fence line; some blood had dried. His hands were icy cold and discolored. He wasn't conscious to answer any questions.

"Let's get him home." Dad propped him between us on the truck seat.

"We've got to get him to a doctor," I said. "Drive to the hospital."

"We'll wake up your momma and get Twitch on the phone. Maybe your momma has a number for that new doctor, Doctor Jacks." Dad drove down the middle of the road. He kept one hand on the steering wheel and with the other hand he helped me hold Ricky upright between us. The drive to our farm only took minutes but seemed an eternity at the same time. My bare hands were covered in blood and my clothes were soaked in blood.

"He might have internal injuries," I said.

"He probably does. That's why we're going to stabilize him at home instead of bouncing him around in this truck for two hours."

I didn't agree with Dad's decision, but I let him lead me. Let Momma chew his butt if she thought he was wrong.

DAD CARRIED RICKY in his arms like a baby while I held the door to the house open. Dad placed Ricky on the couch. "Now, go get your momma and call Twitch!" He shooed me from the room.

Momma's snoring stopped the moment I opened her bedroom door. She bolted upright from beneath her floral comforter. Her C-Pap mask was askew like a drunken scuba diver. She skinned off the ineffectual mask without turning off the machine. The mask and hose skittered along the floor blowing hair and dust into the air. Momma stomped on the hose like she was killing a snake. Her hair was wrapped around a half dozen pink sponge rollers.

"What is it?" she said.

"Momma, you have to get dressed and help Dad. It's Ricky. I think he is dying."

"Ricky?" She bounded out of the bed, pulled on gray sweatpants, and tucked her pink nightie into the elastic waistband. "Where is he?"

"In the living room."

Momma grabbed her medical bag as she forced her swollen feet into pink fuzzy bunny slippers. Her fuchsia toenails poked out the open toes of her slippers. I knew Ricky had painted those toenails earlier in the week. They looked good. *He's an artist.*

Dad had covered Ricky with a heavy quilt Momma's mom had stitched together with used potholders knitted by BOCK—the Brides of Christ's Kingdom—a group at church. That thing must have felt like a lead vest on his broken body. Dad stroked Ricky's hair and told him he'd be all right.

A low moan left Momma's mouth when she saw Ricky. Her eyes clouded with tears, but she didn't give herself the luxury of sentimentality. She went into nurse mode. She examined the extent of his injuries. I left her to it and called Twitch from the kitchen.

No answer on his house or cell phone, but he picked up when I called the emergency number for his vet service.

"What are you doing at the clinic so late?" I asked.

"It's a big, unflattering story, daughter," he said. "Why're you up so late?" He slurred his words. He called me daughter for the first time I'd ever heard.

Crap. "Are you drunk?"

"Not as drunk as I'm going to be. Are you checking up on me?"

"No, that's not my job. I don't suppose you're safe to drive?"

"Safer to drive than to walk in this condition." He laughed at his own joke.

"Somebody hurt Ricky, bad. Would you get some bandages together, some antiseptics, IV fluids, and injection painkiller—whatever you think a bad beating might require."

Silence.

"Did you hear what I said?"

Then he asked, "Did he say who did it?"

"Not yet. He's unconscious. Just please get that stuff together and I'll come pick you up."

"I'll drive," he said. "That's faster."

"Yeah, that's stupid! You aren't driving. We lost Becky. It doesn't look good for Ricky. I'm tired of losing people over stupid ideas. Stay where you are until I get there."

I told Momma and Dad I'd pick up Twitch. I didn't share the details of his intoxicated condition.

ON THE WAY to Twitch's clinic I thought about Ricky, of course. *Who hurt him? Why?* I had worried he would get hurt at the Lake Tavern. Who would have the hate to strip, beat, and tie him to a fence to bleed to death? I couldn't believe anything so cruel could happen in my hometown. Maybe I deluded myself. It had happened other places.

The vet clinic was a store front on Main Street sandwiched between the library and Implement Shop. Its oversized front window read, *Bend Veterinary Clinic*, with some paintings of our three dogs and some cats and sheep I didn't recognize. Charity had done the lettering and paintings for Twitch the first year we were together. It seemed like a lifetime ago. Now it seemed like she was away from Bend more and more. Just seeing the painting tugged my heart and gave me sensations other places I didn't have time to think about. I was ashamed for thinking of myself when Ricky suffered.

When I entered the vet clinic a bell tinkled above my head. The security lights Twitch installed bathed the room in a sickly yellow light. The odor of recent beer and strong perfume wafted into my face. I flipped on the big overhead light.

Twitch cussed and covered his eyes. He sat in his desk chair. He grumbled a little more. Then he rummaged through the drawers of his desk. Dressed in only an undershirt and his jeans with the Superman emblem on the belt buckle, he pulled a clean sweatshirt over his head. A dirty blood-stained shirt lay balled up on top of the desk. He grabbed it and threw it to the floor at his feet.

"What happened to you?" I didn't wait for his answer. He'd need to take a number for my sympathies right then. I snatched the bag of supplies he had gathered and packed in a box by his feet. I headed back to my truck. Twitch must've been satisfied with his clothes and supply packing. He followed me to my truck and sat slumped back against the passenger seat.

"I'm sorry, Lorraine," Twitch said. *Burp.* "I'm sorry you had to come get me and see me like this."

"Are you going to throw up?"

"Not yet. How's Ricky?" Twitch didn't look at me. "Is he talking yet?"

"I don't know. He's unconscious. His face is a mess. Some of his clothes were gone." I concentrated on the road, but snuck glances at Twitch.

"You think he found a boyfriend? Christ." Twitch sort of laughed and shifted in his seat.

"What I saw wasn't about dating. He took a beating."

"It's no surprise. He's been asking for something like this to happen."

"What do you mean?" I nearly swerved off the road.

"He's been at the Lake Tavern every weekend for weeks now and God knows what other beer joints. Kenny and that Russ thought it was funny to bring that goof along. Not everybody thought it so amusing."

Twitch being my biological dad was the result of an ill-advised one-night stand between him and Momma. I'd never been ashamed of the fact until that moment. Right then, I wished I didn't know Twitch was my blood.

"What are you saying? He deserved a beating because he's gay and went to a beer joint?"

"Well, no. I mean, you had to have seen him prance around, Lorraine. Guys aren't comfortable with that sort of behavior." Twitch gave a limp wrist gesture. He was digging himself a big hole, but too drunk to give up the digging.

"What behavior? Drinking? Dancing?"

"Not just that, but you know, looking at guys and being friendly."

"Oh, so he deserved a beating because he looked at guys and was friendly?"

"You're twisting my words, Lorraine. I'm too drunk to explain myself very well."

"I think you being drunk keeps you from hiding what you really think. It's good to know. By your logic I'd deserve the same beating if I was at a beer joint, danced, or seemed friendly to women."

"No. You don't deserve no beating. That's a different thing. You don't flaunt yourself."

"You're right, Twitch. Charity and I don't flaunt ourselves. We try not to be noticed. God forbid anybody feeling uncomfortable around the queers."

"Don't talk like that." Twitch stroked his hair back roughly like he wanted to pull it from his head.

I could see his suffering, but I didn't let him off the hook. "Does the word queer hurt your feelings or is it that you can't imagine two women or two men can fuck? Is that what makes you all squirmy and uncomfortable?"

"Stop, Lorraine."

"Charity and I do our fucking in secret. Guess it's something we have in common, don't we, Dad?"

"Stop, Lorraine! Just stop, God damn you!"

"I'm told God probably will damn me." I drove the truck up our long drive and flattened the edge of Little Man's plastic sandbox.

"I'll quit talking about it for right now, but if you and I are going to have any type of real relationship we're going to need to talk this through." In for a penny, in for a pound, so I kept going. "You can't stop me or Ricky from being who we are, and neither can the sick bastard who beat him. You can ignore us, tolerate us, hate us, legislate us to your heart's content, but you can't stop us. My dad once told me, 'Nobody controls who we love.'"

I took the bag of supplies from the truck. I didn't wait to make sure Twitch staggered to the house. I heard him retch in the grass as I opened the screen door.

Chapter Twelve

I FUMED AS I unpacked the supplies from Twitch's office. Momma grabbed at bits and pieces of it as quickly as I put it down.

"Lorraine, Lorraine, are you listening?" Dad grabbed my arm.

"Yes, I'm listening. Did Momma call Doctor Jacks?"

"No, she said he's probably been drinking at the tavern or elsewhere and isn't fit for providing medical aid." Dad went on to tell me Momma had catalogued Ricky's condition by phone to a doctor at the hospital in Langston. By a conservative estimate Ricky had a broken jaw which Momma had immobilized with a pair of pantyhose tied up around his head. I prayed to God they were new pantyhose so Ricky didn't have to breathe the smell of sweat and secretions that could get caught in that awful invention once it had been worn. He'd already suffered more than enough.

Ricky probably had a concussion, broken ribs, too many cuts and abrasions to count, and likely internal bleeding and ruptures that couldn't be confirmed until he underwent x-rays and more poking and prodding at a hospital.

Based on the phone consultation, Momma injected Ricky with some morphine Twitch had. She inserted an IV drip of fluids and splinted his broken fingers with tape and tongue depressors. I helped Momma cut away the rest of Ricky's clothing. We cleaned and dabbed antiseptic creams on the cuts and scratches and wrapped him in clean bedsheets.

Dad blew up the air mattress with the air compressor. He put the mattress by the station wagon. He made a quick assessment of Twitch, shook his head, and turned back to me. Dad asked me to help carry Ricky out of the house. Momma trailed behind us with the IV bag. We placed him on the mattress and slid him, air mattress and all, into the back of the station wagon. Momma hung the IV bag from the Jesus bar. It was a cozy nest considering the circumstances.

The seats down in the station wagon left room for only a driver and passenger in the car with Ricky. Momma sat in the passenger seat, but she had Ricky's head within reach so she could monitor his breathing and pet his head on the way to the hospital. No room for me. I suggested I could drive separately, but Momma reminded me that Allan needed minding.

"What about Kenny?" I asked. "He's his dad."

"Kenny's not home yet," Momma said through the car window as Dad drove away from the house. "I don't know where the boy is."

What in the hell? Twitch had stopped retching, but I sure as hell wasn't going to offer to drive him home or trust him to take proper care of Allan if he woke up in the night.

I went upstairs in disbelief that Kenny hadn't come home yet. Maybe he'd got a ride with somebody else. No Kenny. Allan slept sprawled out on his side of the bed. No evidence of anyone having wrinkled the other side where Kenny usually slept. I checked Ricky's room. His posters of male bodybuilders and the color wheel of hair dye stared back at me from the empty room. No Kenny bunking there either. I checked my room. I don't know why I bothered. Maybe I just couldn't believe that fool, Kenny, was AWOL when our family needed him. I went back downstairs.

Bottles clinked together as Twitch found two Grain Belts in the toilet tank where Momma usually hid them. He sat at the table, opened them both, but didn't offer either one to me.

"I'm going to drink these and then fall asleep on the couch over there until your dad gets home and can take me home. Any objections?"

I shook my head. I wanted to tell him I hoped he drowned on the beer, but I gave him the silent treatment instead. When that lost its appeal, I went back upstairs, undressed, and took over Kenny's room with Allan. Wherever the hell Kenny ended up, he could just find somewhere else to sleep. He should have been home. It gnawed at me. I supposed he was with Ramona again. They'd done something together or with Allan once and sometimes twice every week since they'd met. I worried it was only a matter of days before Kenny wouldn't come home at all and it meant he might take Little Man away. Damn it. Allan. Allan. Allan. I crawled in bed with Allan.

I didn't expect to sleep. The thought of sleeping scared me because I figured the nightmares of Becky's death would now be a double feature with what I saw when Dad and I found Ricky. *What does it mean? Becky died. Ricky's beaten? These are movies of the week, put it on Jerry Springer type events. How could they happen to our family in Bend, Minnesota? Ricky was just hanging there in front of the car lights. Somebody hurt him and left him there. Somebody wants him dead.*

The adrenaline must have worn off because surprisingly, I slept. I also dreamed.

First, I had the sweet sensation of stroking silky hair, but the dream changed. I felt hand on my hip as I slept on my side. Then a body pressed up against the length of me—spooning me. Warm breath tickled my neck just ahead of a cool nose nuzzled below my ear. I dreamed. I turned. I expected to lace my arms around Charity and find Charity's lips with my mouth.

Screams pulled me from my sweet dream. First my screams, then Kenny's screams, and then Allan's screams.

"What are you doing?"

"What are you doing?"

"I was sleeping until you attacked me."

"Attacked you? I didn't attack you. I rolled over in my bed."

"Why were you up against me like that?"

"Like what? Why are you in my bed? That's a better question in my book."

"You barely know how to read a book."

"That's low, Lorraine." Kenny stood up.

I noticed he was naked and had an erection, but that disturbed me less than what I noticed next. His eye was bruised and his lip was swollen. I shifted across the bed and grabbed his hands and examined his knuckles. They were scraped and swollen.

"Oh, Kenny! You didn't!"

"Didn't what?" He pulled his hands away and took the corner of the sheet to cover himself. It looked like Pinocchio playing at being a ghost.

"Did you beat him?"

"I wouldn't really say I beat him. I hit him a few times and his balls are going to be sore for a long while." Kenny laughed.

"Oh Kenny, why?" I wanted to weep.

"Why? It was him or me. The bastard choked me and would've finished the job if I hadn't kicked him in the balls."

"He's so little—there's no way he could overpower you."

"Kicked him in the balls," Allan said. "Dad, can Raine sleep with us every night?"

"No!" Kenny and I said in unison.

"Put some clothes on. I can't talk to you when you are all hanging out like that."

"Don't boss me. You're not my mother or my wife." He dropped the sheet. "This is my room. I'll hang out if I want." His penis no longer saluted.

"Fine."

"Fine."

Allan held the covers up and peeked inside his underpants. "I'll hang out if I want."

"I just can't believe you could do something like this to Ricky," I said.

"Ricky?" Kenny scoffed. "I don't know how it's any skin off Ricky's ass!"

"Real funny, Kenny."

"Real funny, Dad," Allan mimicked.

"It won't be so funny when the sheriff comes looking for you for assault or murder if he dies."

Kenny laughed. "That coward won't dare press charges."

I flew at Kenny. What I lacked in technique I made up for in the surprise of the attack. I took him to the floor and beat him with my fists which for some odd reason caused Kenny to get hard again. Jeesh.

All of a sudden Momma and Dad were upstairs. *They're home. How's Ricky?*

"Grandpa!" Allan ran to Dad. Momma, who had such a one-track mind about getting me matched up to a boy, misread the whole situation.

"Praise God, my prayers have been answered. Oh, oh, we'll just leave you two alone. Come on, Allan. Your dad and Lorraine are going to pray together."

"We are not."

"She's trying to kill me!" Kenny pointed at me.

Dad moved in front of Momma. "Hey, Allan will you help me out? Will you go feed the dogs?"

Allan ran out.

"Peggy, will you help Allan? I'll stay here with the kids and sort out their religious experience." He giggled himself into a coughing fit, but still guided Momma out of the bedroom by the shoulders.

Momma called back over her shoulder, "Just so you two know. I'm fine with you being in love."

Dad closed the door once Momma left and scrutinized me.

"I hate him!" I said.

"Well, I hate you back!" Kenny crossed his arms in front of him.

"What in the blue blazes has gotten into you two? I've made one trip to the hospital tonight and I don't plan to make another."

Kenny turned to Dad. "Why were you at the hospital?"

"Like you don't know." I kicked him in the shin but got the worst end of the deal because I was barefoot.

"She's possessed."

"Lorraine, sit over there, cover yourself." Dad pointed me to the bed and then directed Kenny. "Kenny, put on some pants."

I scanned myself in just in a T-shirt and panties. I'd never been so exposed around Kenny. I was prepared to fight him in clothes, naked, or in a scuba suit. It didn't matter to me.

"Dad, Kenny beat Ricky!"

"He did what?"

Kenny had only one leg in his jeans.

Dad shoved him and he fell back to the floor. "You beat that boy?" Dad started coughing. "How could you?"

"This family is all crazy!" Kenny yelled.

That remark didn't sit well with Dad or me considering Becky had killed herself during a psychotic episode. Dad lunged for Kenny's throat and I bit the first part of him I reached—his shoulder.

"Ouch! Stop that! I didn't hurt Ricky!" Kenny wheezed before Dad completely choked off his air supply.

"What?" I wiped my mouth and pried Dad's hands away from Kenny's throat. "You said you hit him."

Dad let go of Kenny.

"I never hit Ricky. I hit Russ."

Dad reached for Kenny's shoulder. "You hit Russ?"

I socked Kenny in the gut. "Why'd you hit Russ?"

"Why'd you think I hit Ricky?"

"Somebody beat Ricky," Dad told Kenny.

"Well, Ricky was still roaming the Tavern when Ramona and I left and believe me, he was feeling no pain."

"So, who beat Ricky?" I asked.

Kenny shrugged. "I don't know."

"Why'd you hit Russ?" I didn't hit him.

He lowered his eyes like he was sad or ashamed. "I'd rather not say."

I waved my hand at the bite on his shoulder and the red marks on Kenny's neck. "After all this, you better say."

Kenny pushed himself into a sitting position and put his other leg in his trousers.

"I've been over visiting Ramona. I was a perfect gentleman, Mister Tyler."

"Yeah, I know what a perfect gentleman you can be. Dad, did you know Kenny and Becky even had sex in the concession stand by the football field?"

"Yeah, well ask your daughter how she knows that. She knows because she flunked as a chaperone, but she aced spying on us like a pervert."

I flew at him again, but Dad deflected me and pushed Kenny to the floor again.

"Jesus Christ," Kenny said. "If somebody knocks me on my ass one more time I'm going to..."

"Watch your language!" Dad and I said in unison.

"Okay, okay, truce!" Dad said. "Nobody touch anybody. Let's sort this out."

We were all on the bedroom floor.

"Kenny, you hit Russ?" Dad nodded for Kenny to go on with his story.

"Yes."

"Tell us why."

"I'm afraid you're going to throttle me again or let her bite me." Kenny cast his eyes at Dad.

"You're safe, son, just tell us what happened."

"I left the Tavern at ten and went to see Ramona. Russ came home about midnight or a little after—he'd still been at the Lake Tavern when I left. Anyway, he was already in a foul mood, but got really mad—I guess because I me and Ramona were taking up the TV."

"What show?" I tested him.

"I don't know," Kenny said.

"Figures."

"It was Clint Eastwood and he had Asian neighbors. Can I keep going?" Kenny asked.

"*Gran Torino*. I liked that movie," Dad said. "It's a bit white man as savior for me, but I liked it."

I gave Dad an impatient stare. Movie reviews could wait. "Kenny, go ahead with your story."

"Russ came home from the Tavern already pissed off," Kenny said. "He said something like, 'Why're you still here? Don't you have a son to take care of?' He said it real snotty. I tried to joke with him, but he got nastier and said I had it easy. I could have whatever I wanted. Then he tried to punch me."

"Then what happened?" Dad asked.

"You kicked him in the balls."

"Yeah, I kicked him in the balls and punched him once, maybe twice—just so he wouldn't come after me again. Just look at my eye and my lip. I won't be able to..." He stopped himself. *Probably thought I'd bite him again if he mentioned not being able to kiss Ramona for a week because of a swollen lip. Poor baby.*

"And Ricky was at the Tavern when you left?" Dad asked.

"The place was pretty well packed. Did something happen to Ricky? He drank quite a bit, but he seemed in control of himself and having a good time."

"Somebody beat him up and tied him to the wooden fence by that approach west of the County line." Dad averted his eyes and swallowed hard like just saying it made him feel like throwing up.

"Shit, I don't believe it."

"Lorraine and I went looking for him. Somebody called here and said Ricky was in trouble. I don't know how they knew about it or if they did it themselves. I was half asleep. I don't know if I'd have recognized the voice in daylight, but I sure as hell didn't recognize the voice on the phone in the middle of the night. We found his car and then we found him—he's barely alive."

"Is he going to be all right?" Kenny looked sick.

"I don't know," Dad said. "His jaw's broke, some ribs are broken, his fingers are broke; he took a hell of a beating besides getting stabbed with something. He hadn't yet regained consciousness when Peggy and I left the hospital."

There was a church-like silence for a while.

Kenny surveyed me. "Jeez, Lorraine, you thought I could do that to Ricky?"

Embarrassment pinched my ass, but Kenny's the last person I'd admit that to. "Oh, come on, don't look so wounded. A few years back I thought you killed my sister and buried her in your yard. My trust in you has grown appreciably even with this mistake." I did feel badly about using violence. "I'm sorry I bit you."

"I'm sorry I tried to strangle you," Dad said as he got off the floor. "Well, I better go tell Peggy what I know. Her eavesdropping ability has been put to the test on this one. Come down when you're decent. Kenny, I'll need you to make a list of everybody you saw at the Tavern last night. Sheriff's going to want that once I call him."

"Yes, sir." Kenny flinched when Dad came toward him. "You aren't going to knock me down again, are you?"

"No, son." He hugged Kenny in the A-frame sort of way men hug each other so they don't appear queer. Then he hugged me with the same A-frame hug dads use on their daughters once their daughters get breasts and their period.

I pulled him tight. *I hope you know you're my anchor. All this...all this how could I bear it?* After I let him go, I would've followed him out, but Kenny grabbed my arm.

"Lorraine, I'm sorry about my dream. I didn't know you were in the bed—then I had this dream. It was so real. I could even smell her, you know?"

"Ramona?"

"No. Becky. You're so much alike and you take care of Little Man."

Nobody ever talked about Becky and me being alike.

"Sometimes, I sort of forget she's gone and then I remember...I miss her all over again. I don't think that'll ever go away."

"Maybe the way we feel about our first love never goes away."

"Maybe. That's what I'm afraid of. Maybe I'll never be able to let Becky go enough to love somebody else. I mean, Ramona is great, but..."

"But what? Becky is gone. Nobody knows that better than us. Sometimes, there is no other choice but to move on because our first love isn't there for us anymore."

Against my nature, but I hugged the big goof. His bare chest was smooth against my face. He hugged me back—no A-frame poor excuse for a hug. Our fronts made contact and we held each other tight. I suppose we clung to each other for all we'd lost and maybe even for the future losses we anticipated. *Kenny lost the love of his life. Am I about to learn how that feels?* Then we let go.

Chapter Thirteen

I CALLED CHARITY over and over, but her cell went to voicemail and I became tired of leaving messages that didn't seem to warrant a return call. I wanted to go visit Ricky straight away. Dad said not to, but I didn't listen. I went to the hospital, bought an overpriced mylar balloon of Mickey Mouse at the gift shop, and found Ricky's room. Ricky slept deeply like Dad described, but he was in a medically induced coma, not regular sleep like he did sometimes on the couch at the farm. I laughed to myself thinking of him hugging his pillow and drooling all over his Wonder Woman pillowcase.

In the hospital bed he was flat on his back with tubes poking out of him keeping the balance of fluids coming and going.

"Ricky, I love your yellow purse!" *He'd die to see himself with a catheter bag.* I immediately hated myself for having that thought. *Don't die.*

"Ricky, I don't know the rules for this. Should I update you about your condition? I don't even know if you can hear me." *Act as if, Lorraine. He's your friend and he needs to talk with you, or at least hear you talk.*

"You never were much for pregnant silences. If it were me in that bed you'd be jabbering about something or telling me how to look better. Don't worry, I won't try to cosmetologize you. I don't know how, but I can tell you about your body. I'm almost a vet, you know."

I sat on a chair I pulled up to his bed. "Well, your makeup is overdone. That is to say you've got some bruising." *This is dumb. I sound like a fool.*

What else? "It might feel a bit discombobulating that you've got all these bandages and tubes, but you aren't in any pain. The pain is there. You're just doped up pretty good so you don't have to manage all the pain signals your body is sending out. If we could show you your pain signals it would look like one of those TV weather maps when a big storm is going through. You don't need that." I gave the room a once-over. There were a couple of bouquets of carnations. *That's what smells like the funeral home.* Somebody had brought magazines. *Maybe I can read to him next time.*

"They x-rayed you and taped up your broken ribs. There's splints on your fingers. Lucky for me I guess or you'd be trying to fix my hair." *Lost cause.*

"Good news is they've detected no internal bleeding. Infection is still a risk. I'm guessing part of the cocktail going into your veins is some antibiotics. They stitched you up in a few places." *I'm not saying anything about scars. He doesn't need to worry about still being pretty.*

I scratched my head. "Obviously, you got hit in the noggin hard enough to break your jaw, but the doctor's saying there's no signs of brain bleed or swelling. That's really important information and if you don't remember a word of what I'm saying remember it's good news that there's probably no brain damage." *You idiot. That's not the most important thing. Tell him you love him and everybody loves him—not the person who did this obviously, but most others.*

It felt stupid. All that talking and him not talking back, but I kept going. "Once your jaw swelling goes down they'll surgically repair your jaw. Boy, howdy, I bet you will talk up a storm then." *Will you tell us who did this? Will you want to live somewhere there are people who'd do this?*

I leaned closer and whispered into his ear. His dark hair brushed against my lips. "Ricky, they're going to find out who did this to you and there'll be justice. I promise." I didn't know how exactly I could keep that promise. All I could do is tell what I knew. I left the hospital to meet Dad and our local law enforcement.

BEND, LIKE MOST small towns in Minnesota, had multiple churches and hardware stores, but didn't have money or the level of crime for either a municipal police force or a private security company. The County rationed law enforcement which usually meant a deputy drove through Bend on Sunday morning. Depending on the Sheriff's Department wasn't like the movies where a highly skilled investigator from the crime-ridden metropolis came to a quiet town to exorcise his personal demons, but also solve every local crime with speed, new technology, and old fashioned keen deduction. Bend depended on Sheriff Scrogrum.

Sheriff Scrogrum hadn't been too helpful when Becky went missing, but he got points for being sensitive enough to our family when she died. He had some law enforcement training from the technical college. I didn't doubt his motivation to keep the peace and solve crime, but I'd heard he was sheriff because his dad had been sheriff before him and no one challenged his election. Bend had not benefitted from a competition amongst a pool of competent, ambitious law enforcement candidates. Sheriff Scrogrum had been elected by his friends and neighbors and he in turn recruited some local nitwits to be his deputies. Although I had my doubts he would accomplish much in investigating Ricky's assault, Dad and I agreed to meet him at the spot where we'd found Ricky.

Daylight should have made the scene less scary. Ricky no longer hanging on the fence should have made the place less eerie, but it creeped me out. It helped being with Dad, but then again, I had been with Dad the night before. Just another abhorrent shared experience for the Tyler family.

The sheriff's cruiser blocked the approach where we had left Ricky's car. Either someone had turned off the lights or the battery died. Bright yellow crime scene tape crisscrossed the approach begging for attention, but my eyes kept going back to the fence. The tape was the sheriff's attempt to protect the crime scene Dad and I had already contaminated the night before.

We got out of the truck and walked closer. The gravel crackled under my feet. Cicadas whined. I didn't remember the sound from before, but I suppose my hearing was less alert than my vision. The grasses along the ditch were overgrown. The County hadn't sent the man around with the tractor and cutter to mow the country ditches yet. Coneflowers and wild daisies splashed some color over the neutral browns and greens. *I never want to see the color red again.*

I looked at the fence, the wooden gate where Ricky was tied. It was made of ordinary board. It wasn't a sturdy steel gate. Some of the boards were worn, flaking like dry turkey breast. It wasn't a big gate. It appeared wobbly like it wouldn't hold against much pressure. Some places the boards shone burgundy-brown like rust in contrast to the weather-beaten gray of the boards without blood soaked in. The field had been planted in hay. That would have to be cut down and gathered again later in summer.

"Lorraine, Lorraine." Dad touched my sleeve. "It's time to tell the sheriff what we saw."

Two other official-looking men were with Sheriff Scrogrum—all three men were dressed in poop-brown pants and drab tan shirts and Mountie hats so stiff they'd likely hold water.

"Who's with the sheriff?" I leaned in and kept my voice low. Dad didn't know who they were, but he made a few guesses and I added a few theories I entertained. "Hmm, I wonder who they are."

A voice came from my right. "That would be Mumble and Shuffle."

I startled to find Marin England, the social worker, standing beside me.

"Who? What are you doing here?" *Does she ever not look beautiful? How does she end up in the middle of things?* A wave of embarrassment washed over me as I realized I registered excitement in seeing her again.

"I don't actually know their real names," Marin said. "I've heard about them—nicknamed Mumble and Shuffle. Brothers I think. They are on loan to the County for a year."

"No kidding? Don't tell me they're here to learn from Scrogrum. They must be really dumb."

"I think it is the other way around," Marin said. "They're here to offer some services to the Sheriff's department. They're on loan from the State Crime Lab."

Dad put his hand out to Marin. "Hi, I'm Joseph Tyler, I'm sorry my daughter temporarily forgot her manners.

I'm Lorraine's dad and Ricky has been living at our farm. Lorraine and I were the ones who found him early this morning."

Marin took his hand and introduced herself. "I'm Marin. I work for the County. It's good you found him and got him help. I understand from the hospital that he nearly died." She excused herself and walked over to the sheriff who handed her some papers.

"She seems to know you." Dad bumped his hip against me.

"Yeah, she's the one who picked up Addie from our place."

"Seems nice enough. Pretty woman." He glanced over at Marin and back at me.

I glared at him. *What's his point?* I wasn't ready to process women with Dad. That was even creepier than having cuddled with Kenny. I changed the subject. "Why the nicknames? And why is that social worker here?"

"Let's find out." Dad and I moved closer to the cordoned off area where the sheriff put labels on ziplocked evidence bags. Some of them held shreds of Ricky's clothing, his jeans, part of his good shirt. I spied something black in one of the bags. When I got closer I recognized Ricky's missing shoe. His feet were covered in the hospital. Were his feet hurt too? I looked at the clock on my phone. Was anyone with him while he slept now? The shoe looked lonely and small.

"Joseph, Lorraine, thanks for coming out this morning. I'm going to ask you to stay on the outside of the tape and answer a few questions about what you found." Then the sheriff pointed in the direction of the other two. "That's Billy and Kurt—investigators on loan from the State Crime Lab. They don't mind if you call 'em Mumble and Shuffle. I'm not certain which is which."

Typical. Sheriff Scrogrum can't even solve the mystery of a nickname.

"Hey, you two, this is the party who found that boy tied to the fence," Sheriff Scrogrum yelled in the direction of the two men.

Mumble and Shuffle glanced up from the ground they were studying. They scanned Dad and me. One of them grunted something. The taller one grumbled some more and took out a long skinny notebook and walked toward us. The shorter one followed along behind—a little too close to the first one to take full strides.

"I'm Billy. This here is Kurt. He wants to know how you knew to look here for your friend?"

"We didn't exactly," Dad said. "We got an anonymous tip. Somebody called the house and said Ricky's in trouble up by the County Line and needed help."

Kurt said something to Billy. "You're right," Billy said. "I'll get an order for those phone records ASAP." He nodded at us. "Go on."

"We just drove along the road and saw Ricky's car parked in the approach—lights on. We pulled off and then saw Ricky." Dad's words trailed off. He wiped his eyes with his red bandana. "Christ, what an awful mess."

Mumble grunted some more and Shuffle translated for him. "Can you tell us anything about who called you?"

"Not much, I'd been dead to the world," Dad said. "Sounded like a man, but I didn't recognize his voice and he didn't offer his name."

"Time?"

"A little past 1:00 a.m."

"How'd you see anything?"

"It was dark, but there was a moon." Dad shifted uneasily. "Like I said, his car lights pointed at the fence. Our eyes adjusted and we saw him."

God how I wished I could unsee it. My eyes went back to the gate expecting Ricky's scarecrow while his blood stained the fence and dirt.

Grunt.

"You smoke?"

"Yep, on occasion."

Mumble held out his hand to Dad. In it were three cigarette butts.

"Not my brand. Those have filters," Dad said. "You think whoever beat Ricky left those?"

Grunt.

"Could be. Could be they were here for a couple days—not likely though. It rained night before last. These cigarettes are dry, unstained. Menthol—see here it says Salem." Shuffle then turned his attention to the fence.

"Only one person tied the ropes—same knots on both sides. Could have been more than one who done the beating." Shuffle fanned through the papers on his clipboard and pulled out a ziplock bag. "Found this condom on the ground by the car."

Grunt.

Shuffle continued. "Of course, we'll have to wait for the medical report to know all what happened to that boy."

Despite what he said, I'm guessing he knew very well what we all suspected happened to Ricky. Mumble fished a brown vinyl case out of the sheriff's cruiser. He took out a camera and began photographing things from every angle. He even took a picture of Dad and me. After he scaled one of the large wooden posts of the gate he took pictures looking down where Ricky had been tied. From the top of that post Mumble grunted something at Shuffle and the little minion walked over to Ricky's car, opened the door, and inspected the driver's side.

"God damn if you aren't right!" Shuffle flashed a look at Mumble. Mumble grunted and jumped off the post. Then he went to the car and took some more pictures.

"That boy didn't drive his car here. The seat is all the way back, but not reclined. He couldn't have reached the pedals. It means whoever drove was taller than Ricky and may have left some identifying information in the car. Anybody here touch the inside of the car?" Shuffle eyed each of us, daring us to admit having messed up evidence.

"Nope. Me neither. I'll get a fingerprinting kit and see what I can find." Shuffle started back to the cruiser, but Mumble grunted again. Shuffle turned back to us. "We're going to need your fingerprints to eliminate you. We'll try to get prints on as many people as we can and hope we find something here to compare them to."

Maybe Mumble and Shuffle were good at their job. I looked at my hand, my fingerprints. I balled up my fist and released it quickly like I'd said a swear in church. Mumble grunted something that sounded like, "Howdy piggedy homely."

"How did that other fella or fellas get home? Probably somebody followed Ricky and whoever drove Ricky's car. The one with Ricky maybe left with the other fella or maybe he walked home," said Shuffle.

Mumble went over the fence and peered off in the distance. Then he grunted.

"Who lives at the farms closest to this fence line if you go cross country?" Shuffle asked.

An odd silence sucked the oxygen out of the air. Then Dad answered, "That's the Hollister place—but no one's living there presently. Kenny and his son live with us and his ma got a place in town. The next farm belongs to Gerry Narrows and just beyond her farm is our place."

"You don't say?" Shuffle scribbled in his notebook.

"I do say and I'm not afraid of having you know it. Nobody at any of those places would have ever hurt Ricky. He's like family to us," Dad said. "I'll give you my fingerprints, DNA, and a stool sample if you need it to believe me."

Shuffle eyed his partner. "Are we to understand that this boy who was, as you say, 'like family' was of the homosexual persuasion?"

"Well, I don't know that..." Dad mumbled.

There's no time for more secrets or apologies. "Yep, I don't think anyone persuaded him. He was just born gay," I said. "I am too. What's your point?"

"The point is that maybe your friend's beating related to his sexuality," Shuffle said. "Maybe this is what we'd call a hate crime."

"It sure looked to me like whoever did that to Ricky had a lot of hate in them," I said.

Nobody could argue the point.

"So, it may've been a motive for the beating," Shuffle said. "For now, we're going to gather all the physical evidence we can find and get witness statements from you two and people who were at the bar last night. That's what we can do while we wait for Ricky to tell us what he remembers. May have been a motorist in a passing car saw something." He looked at Mumble and around us at Dad's truck. "We need to know how the assailants got here and how they left. Maybe it was the taller man who was driving his car who hurt him." Mumble went into motion. He climbed over the fence rail and walked and weaved in a fan-shaped pattern.

"What's he doing?" I asked Shuffle.

"If somebody walked off that way, Mumble might find some evidence to help figure out who he was. Mumble can find signs of people they didn't even know they left."

The words were barely out of his mouth when a garbled call came from Mumble.

"What did he say?" asked Dad.

"He's found a boot print and used chewing gum—spearmint he thinks. He wants the plaster cast making kit and another couple plastic bags. Damn, he's good." Shuffle went to the cruiser and got the equipment Mumble requested.

I'd forgotten about Marin until she touched my arm.

"Did Ricky say anything about who did this to him?" she asked.

"What would it matter? I told you McGerber's a creep and he's still walking around like King Shit."

"Lorraine, don't be rude." Dad turned to Marin. "Ricky wasn't even conscious. Say, how did that business come out with Addie? She okay?"

"She is doing well. She's at the horse ranch I told Lorraine about. You should come see her. If you did, she would tell you again that she had a boyfriend. McGerber didn't get her pregnant." Marin turned to me. "I'm here because your friend's going to need some help from the County. He needs medical insurance and maybe even a nursing home when he leaves the hospital. I can help with that. That's my job. I'm good at it. I do it because I care about people and the people who love them."

Maybe Dad would just tape my mouth shut and save us all the embarrassment of the asinine things I say. Shame pinched my ass, both my breasts, my liver and heart to the point of me bowing my head and struggling to talk. "I'm sorry, you're right. Addie told me it wasn't McGerber." I should've apologized more and better, but I wanted to get away. I started to climb the fence. Sheriff Scrogrum edged in front of me.

"You can't go into the field. There could be evidence all through here. I know you folks wouldn't want to compromise our investigation. I have your number and I'll call you if we have any more questions. Thank you."

Before Marin left she handed another business card to me. "In case you lost the other one. I figure you must've lost it or you'd have called me by now."

I took the card and the strong hint. I watched her in her black jeans as she walked away. Even though I'd been a puke, she continued being sweet to me.

"I may be wrong given my age and heterosexual persuasion, but I think that girl seems to want to hear from you, Lorraine," Dad said.

I lightly punched Dad's shoulder when he sniggered on the way to the truck. I wondered if he saw that my relationship with Charity passed away. *Maybe I'm the last to know.*

Chapter Fourteen

DAD SUGGESTING THAT another woman wanted me unsettled me on several levels. I put Marin's business card in my pocket, but as soon as I was back to my own truck, I drove to find Charity. I wanted to tell her about Ricky. I wanted her to assure me that what happened to Ricky was a random thing and no one here in Bend could possibly have done it. I wanted her to tell me we were safe. Hell, I wanted the moon and to be kissing Charity by the light of that moon. Maybe it would stop me from thinking about Ricky—that he might die like Becky did; and somebody was out hunting queers.

Well praise the lord and pass the hotdish. Charity's little red truck was parked in the drive by Grind's tan sedan. The Grinds' tidy white two-story house stood like something out of a story book. The grass had been cut, the front flower beds were weedless and mulched. A cross hung on the oak front door, visible through the beveled oval glass opening of the storm door. I scanned the yard for Charity's dad. I chanced being run off by him if he found me there.

Pastor Grind was occupied, thankfully. He didn't take time to come over and chastise me for being there or warn me against seeing Charity or condemn me for being queer or just being. He sat on a lawn chair with his back to me, oblivious as he jabbered with another man, vaguely familiar, but his face was obscured by the pole of the table umbrella. I couldn't identify him. Mrs. Grind told me to wait on the outside porch and she would get Charity for me. From where I sat I heard bits and pieces of Grind's conversation with the faceless man.

"You've heard about my campaign I assume? I'm sure you have. I'm endorsed by the Traditional Party and mother approved." His voice trailed off, but then he said, "But I have bigger ambition than that."

Words and fragmented sentences filtered back to where I waited for Charity. I heard something like, "If we are going to take this country back...Godly men... purification of America through...word of God... I want... this district... Allister, my campaign wants you...in Bend, Minnesota. Congratulations."

Round two involved trying to make sense of Pastor Grind's words from that distance. "President of... I don't know what to say." I stepped back from the door and peeked at Pastor Grind. He rubbed his neck. I couldn't tell if he was excited or fatigued.

"Allister." The man leaped to his feet. I ducked back nearer the door. I still couldn't see his face, but he spoke louder. "Of course, you'll think about it. Don't take too long, you're the committee's first choice and we're willing to waive half the usual commitment contribution, but there is a Baptist fellow in St. Wendell who received nearly as many votes as you did, and he didn't seem to need the waivered fees. But, as I said previously, you're the committee's first choice."

"Baptist?" Grind spoke louder now and even with his back to me I caught most of what he said. "What is the contribution? What's involved in being president of a local chapter of your campaign?"

In more whispered tones the man continued. I strained to hear what they were saying. Then I heard the man say something like, "Your job is to...a vote for me is a vote for God, family and the values of America."

"When you say meetings..."

I missed a lot of what they said but perked up when I heard the other man say, "Be it evil or a threat to democracy in this community, your church, or own home, I will vanquish it."

I imagined my senior picture in the dictionary next to the entries of this man's notion of evil.

Flat against the siding of the house, I passed the picture window to get a closer look. Pastor Grind nodded like a bobble-headed dog in the back window of a car. I'd heard him preach the exact stuff the man prattled on about, but perhaps Pastor Grind had never been made a president.

The man extricated himself from the lawn chair. "Well, certainly if you need more convincing of the world's need for God, I could drop by some printed materials. I just thought an experienced man of the word like you wouldn't hesitate to heed the call of Jesus and be a leader. If we have misjudged your commitment I'm sincerely sorry. I can withdraw your nomination."

"No, no, don't do that. I am very committed." Pastor Grind searched his pockets and pulled out his checkbook. I imagined Grind's picture by the evils of pride and gullibility in that man's dictionary. "What was the fee you spoke about?"

"A mere five hundred dollars."

Holy crap. Who would want to have to pay five hundred dollars to be president of anything?

As the man pocketed the check he passed a paper to Grind with a list of what he called talking points for his campaign.

I scooted back to my original position by the door. I swallowed hard and knocked for a second time.

Mrs. Grind came to the door again. She was red faced and I suspect she lied to me. She expressed her apologies. Charity was not home. She had left earlier with a friend and Mrs. Grind had forgotten. She'd give her a message that I stopped by when she saw her again. Mrs. Grind closed the door before I could respond. I hustled to my truck as the men walked closer to the house and left.

Chapter Fifteen

I CAN'T SAY I intended to drive there, but suddenly I found myself parked in the approach where Ricky almost died. The crime tape lay on the ground, flapping in the breeze. It had ineffectually cordoned off the area. Not even the deer respected the boundary. Scat, beer bottles, cigarette butts, and candy bar wrappers littered the ground where spectators had visited the scene. In crime shows the perpetrator often returns to the scene of the crime to relive the thrill or even be a helper in the investigation. I wondered if whomever beat Ricky now played helper in some way.

I picked up some of the trash and kicked the scat into the ditch. I coiled the yellow crime tape into a roll and threw it in the back of my truck. From the cab of my truck I stared at the gate. Gates usually lead to something or they hold things in or keep others out. It shouldn't surprise me that Charity wasn't home and stayed away more and more. I'd tried to keep her in Bend. *I'm not moving toward anything new or safeguarding anything. I'm just hanging on the gate going nowhere. I can't expect Charity to wait around for me.* I hit the steering wheel with the heel of my hand. Anger tightened my muscles to the point that I thought my tendons might tear away from my bones. I ground my teeth and screamed, "I'm doing my best!"

I wasn't just biding my time. I had family responsibilities and my family grew when Ricky came to live in our house. What about Addie? Somebody took advantage of her and Grind was listening to some jerk who was more than willing to add yeast to the hate that in this town so far had been left unleavened.

I stared at the gate and then I got out of my truck and kicked the boards loose from it. Every kick hurt my booted foot and vibrated to my spine, but I lay siege to the wooden gate and bashed it until the old boards were stripped off and the frame of it bowed to the ground, straining against the rusting hinges. That gate couldn't keep anything, anyone in or out or just hanging on. The way around was through. There was no purpose in licking my wounds past, present, or future. I had things to do. I headed to town.

SOME WOULD CALL it auto pilot. Somehow my driving was controlled by a deeper part of my brain. I parked in front of the library. If you want to believe in democracy and the Constitution, you've got to respect the library. It's a place anyone can go and belong and get access to anything ever written, maybe even thought. The Bend Library was modest. It shared space in a building that also housed Bend's only dentist office. I suspected the high-pitched whirl of the drills sometimes disturbed the folks thumbing through the periodicals. It wasn't that the forty by thirty-foot room had an impressive collection; it didn't. But whatever was there anybody in Bend could look at it, take most any of it home for a week, and they could order stuff from bigger collections that could be sent there or seen online. There was no requirement to prove you were worthy or educated enough to check something out. Information was not protected or locked away from the common person. There was even a measure of privacy about what each citizen chose to read.

The place looked and smelled the same, a little dusty, a little musty. The same paintings of dead presidents hung on the wall, the one of Washington in a suit relaxing in a bubble bath my favorite. The library would always be special, almost holy to me not just because of the freedom of information there, but because the library was where I first met Charity.

The concrete walls kept the space reasonably cool. Even so, Gerry Narrows, my neighbor and friend, the Bend Community Library librarian, had all the ceiling fans running and an oscillating fan blew right at her from the library counter. She wore her three-piece peach gabardine suit and a white blouse with covered buttons and small embroidered rabbits on it. Gerry had helped me apply to vet school, she'd harbored my sister Becky during her psychotic break, she'd helped me register my momma for nursing school, and she'd kept our family fed as we reeled from the grief of Becky's death. It was probably good that we didn't have much of an appetite. Gerry was a better librarian than she was a cook.

Gerry clattered at the counter, no doubt processing a request for a library card or ordering more books. She didn't notice me until I approached the desk.

"Lorraine Tyler." She came around the library counter and hugged me. "I'm so sorry about your friend, Ricky. How is he doing? How are you doing?"

She smelled like chocolate and peanut butter. Sure enough, there was an open package of peanut butter cups on her work area. "I won't kid you, Gerry. It's been hard.

I don't feel safe and I never thought I'd say that about Bend."

"For good reason. I don't know what this country is coming to."

"I'm hoping you can help me find out a little bit about a stranger in town who seems to be coming to Bend to run for some state office on an agenda of hate."

Gerry took her seat behind her desk and booted up her computer. The screen saver was a collection of flags and the words "Freedom for All" and "Love Always Wins" scrolling over the flags.

"This guy was over at Grind's house talking to Allister about being president of something to do with his campaign."

"Well, did he say what office he was running for? Are we talking this November's election?" Gerry clacked the keys on her computer and opened multiple pages on the internet.

"Sorry, I didn't catch all of it. He said he's endorsed by something called the Traditional Party. Does that help?"

Gerry pounded on the keyboard of her computer like she was running scales on a piano. "Great." She rolled her eyes. "From what I see here the Traditional Party is a puritanical group led mostly by men trying to enforce strict rules on women, children, and whole communities. They distort evangelical Christianity, hide under the flag of nationalism, and worship capitalism and label anything else as evil and unpatriotic. No offense to your friend."

"He's not my friend. Why would Grind hook up with them? Doesn't he get enough opportunity to renounce sin by being a pastor?"

"Well, if what you say is right, he may have felt pressured to do it or his ego told him he should do it. Maybe Grind has some political aspirations himself and is courting the Traditional Party for support."

"Do you think? Wow, I can't imagine him being like...a senator, or God forbid the president. Certainly, no one would be stupid enough to vote for someone as narrow-minded as Grind."

"Those folks who would vote for someone like this man or Grind aren't bad or ignorant people. They are loyal, patriotic, and often very kind generous people who will vote against their self-interests if that vote helps their country or faith. There's plenty of rich, powerful people who will gladly let someone else sacrifice their self-interests if it helps the rich stay rich and powerful stay powerful." She tilted her head. "There's probably some who get goaded and manipulated into being afraid of differences and feeling like they have to support these certain demagogues if they are being faithful to God and country. There can be extremism any place." Gerry covered her mouth with her hand. "Here's some pictures from rallies and town hall meetings. Police have been called to respond to some of these. Oh God."

"What?" I leaned closer to the computer screen.

"This article says that a man was dragged behind a car after coming out of a gay bar in Florida. Members of an ultra-conservative political group were implicated in the hate crime. No charges were ever filed. Says here the man died."

"Print that out. Oh my God, what if that's the group or like the group this guy is representing? Maybe I'm being paranoid or overly dramatic."

The inkjet printer chattered and spit out a copy of the article as Gerry pulled up a list of candidates who had declared their intentions of being candidates for the Minnesota House of Representatives. I scanned the pictures but didn't see anyone who resembled the guy at Grind's place, not that I got much of a clear view of him.

"Maybe he is running for a congressional spot in the next cycle and he hasn't filed yet."

"Maybe. He sure made it sound like he was already in the running. Thanks, Gerry. Will you look at something else with me?"

"You know I will."

I had the roster Kenny had made of everyone he knew who darkened the doors of the Tavern the night Ricky was hurt. I'd made a copy of it for myself before I turned the list over to the sheriff. I took the list from my pocket and flattened it in front of Gerry. "Would anyone on this list strike you as someone who would beat Ricky?"

We reviewed the roster together. The list was long and spotty. I knew it didn't prove anything, but I searched for someone who might be a guy like Grind or of his ilk. It seemed like a good starting place.

Kenny didn't know more than half the people who were there at the beginning of the night and he knew even fewer by the time he left at ten. Kenny named Russ, Twitch, Dr. Jacks, Big Will, Lucille the hairdresser and her husband, Sammy. Kenny listed those who worked at the Tavern too: Tootsie, the short-order cook who would have been a chef a fancy restaurant if she'd left Bend. Cindy waited tables as a second job to get a break from her painting studio. Doris bartended but could easily have run a third world country with efficiency and grace. Ed made popcorn between drawing beers for Doris and slurping Grain Belt as he talked with anyone who sat close enough.

"That place needs a bouncer to manage the characters who drink there."

"You got that right. Dad goes there and so does Kenny and now Ricky and the guys Momma lured over from the junior college." I decided not to add my thought that Gerry would make a great bouncer. "Kenny said there were some men he assumed were farmhands, but he didn't know their names, lots of cabin rental and summertime folks, and some big-mouthed boys in college letter jackets with giggly girlfriends hanging on them. He said those assholes spilled beer on Ramona and that was one of the reasons Kenny and Ramona left early."

"I hate to say it, Lorraine, but it could be anybody—even someone you think you know well."

Of course, I knew that. I just didn't like connecting the dots. I went on with my sleuthing. "The Tavern closed officially at midnight, but it's common knowledge that Ed let people linger and drink longer. Dad and I had found Ricky just after 1:00 a.m. Kenny said he didn't know anything about the older man checking out Ricky other nights they were there."

Gerry scowled and bobbed her head. "We both know the locals and short-timers tend to stay separate past polite conversation—are the fish biting? Where should I go for fresh bait? It would be hard to find out those names."

I peered at the list and wondered how I could narrow down the suspects. I didn't lack incentive or time. Just then my phone chirped.

"Lorraine, are you okay?" Gerry touched my arm.

"Yeah, just disappointed. Charity texted that she doesn't have time to see me. Again. She said she'll write or call."

"You don't seem like you're so sure she will."

I started to text Charity back but abandoned the effort. "I'm sure. She's said it a lot lately, but I haven't heard much from her. It's over."

"Nobody likes being left in relationship limbo." Gerry shook her head. "I'm sorry you're going through all this. I'm no expert, but I've heard it's best to pull the Band-Aid off quick."

"Thanks, Gerry. I know I have to talk to Charity about all this, but she's never around to talk face to face. I am trying to write her a letter, but I haven't found the right words yet. I never told you, but Charity broke up with me by letter once before. Maybe that's why I can't seem to finish the letter."

"Jeez, a breakup letter is cowardly." Gerry gave me a wide-eyed look. "No offense."

"No offense taken. It was a chicken-shit way to break up and it happened when I lost the scholarship and Becky disappeared."

"Ooh, wicked."

I didn't understand how Charity could put me off like a telemarketer. She was an artist who wrote poetry on my underwear the first time we made love. We'd made love more times than I could count (two hundred and fifty-seven times). Her touch had lingered on my skin, but now I was numb and confused. I wished Charity was there to help me. More than that, I wished Charity was there to hold me. *Who am I kidding? It's over. The fat lady sang. Hell, the fat lady was probably Momma.*

I didn't say any of that to Gerry, it was too private, but I did say something I hadn't let myself say to anybody. "Who else can I talk to about Ricky? Those investigators are wondering if this was a hate crime. Who else would understand I'm scared too? Who else in this town knows what it's like to be terrified they're going to be beat up for just being who they are?"

"I understand, Lorraine. Don't think I haven't thought of you when I heard what happened. Don't think I didn't worry you'd take up solving this crime and maybe get hurt yourself." Gerry took both my hands. "Whatever asshole did this may not be satisfied with one beating or he might come back to finish the job."

Tears came to my eyes, my nose ran. I couldn't talk about any of it anymore.

"You can stay at my place, Lorraine."

"Thanks, Gerry. I'll keep that in mind. I think for now I need to be at home. For right now, I need to visit Ricky."

Chapter Sixteen

OPEN YOUR EYES! I wished it, prayed it, and pretended I had the kind of mental telepathy that could make it happen. Who the hell would settle for bending spoons if you could use your power to create medical miracles? I had no special powers. Ricky didn't open his eyes. He couldn't talk even if he was conscious. His jaws were still wired shut and he was being given fluids through a needle in his arm. A feeding tube down his nose was on the horizon. I bet he wouldn't be asking for that recipe once he was well. If he got well.

Most of his fingers were broken so he couldn't write a note. He was a human still life—something to sketch if the artist found distorted features and wasting muscle and flesh captivating. Drawing him made me think of Charity again and a new wave of sadness and regret washed over me.

I read to him from *People* magazine because I knew he'd love the celebrity gossip. I flashed pictures at him pretending he could see the awful hairstyle or the weight gain or weight loss story. I tried to sound upbeat and optimistic rather than how helpless I felt seeing him in the hospital bed. The visiting hours were generous considering Ricky's condition, but the visitors' list was short. Other than his parents and my parents, I was the only nonmedical, non-county worker allowed in his room. I supported the restrictions since we didn't know who had hurt Ricky. I even glimpsed Grind getting turned away by the day nurse, a woman who may have been a prison guard prior to working at Langston hospital.

I squeezed my eyes closed as I pleaded and prayed for Ricky to wake up. My useless meditation was interrupted.

"We have to stop meeting like this." Marin bumped her shoulder against me. "Are you still mad at me about how Addie's case came out or can we be friends?"

My whole face smiled. I looked into her eyes with the same need a plant has when it leans toward sunlight. "Well, since you seem to pop up to help people I care about, we better figure out a way to be friends. What can you do for Ricky?"

Marin smiled too. She pulled the extra chair closer to me. I smelled lavender. "I got his state insurance opened so that his hospital care is covered, his medications, and he can get rehabilitation services after his stay here."

"When he's done here, he's coming to our house," I said. "We have a room set up downstairs. It's the room where Addie stayed. Years ago, I shared that room with my sister, Becky. We have burned sage in there since then. I think any residue of our fights is long gone. Momma and I can take care of Ricky."

"That is a good hearted, generous offer, Lorraine, but because Ricky isn't conscious to speak for himself and hasn't completed any paperwork assigning a medical power of attorney, his parents will need to decide the details of his medical care."

"Will you ever give me any good news?"

"Good news? I have good news. Addie is doing well. She loves the ranch. She'd like to see you again. She said you have a kitten for her."

"I do. Can she have a kitten there?"

"Yeah, why don't you bring it out on Saturday? I'm working there in the morning...I'm off in time for lunch after." She didn't wait for a response. Before I could babble anything, a woman had entered the room and the moment she saw Marin she took her into her arms and kissed her cheek. The woman had a Mayan build and the female equivalent of Ricky's beauty. I knew in an instant this was Ricky's mother.

"Maria, do you know Ricky's good friend, Lorraine Tyler?" Marin asked.

Next the woman had me in an embrace.

"I'm Maria Lopez Johnson," she said. "You are my son's good friend, the daughter of that big woman from his school? Thank you."

"Hi, Mrs. Johnson. I'm really sorry somebody hurt Ricky. My dad and I found him that night."

Marin told Mrs. Johnson she had to go, then she nodded at me. "Until Saturday." She left. I know I stared at the empty space Marin left behind her like something of her presence remained in the room. I startled when I remembered Mrs. Johnson was still there.

I watched as Ricky's mother approached his bedside. "I'm so glad you and your father saved my son." Her coffee-brown hair was braided and reached past her waist. "I bet Ricky liked to play with your hair."

I pulled a chair to the bed and sat beside her. "Oh, yes. He loves my hair. He knows how to do hair."

Mrs. Johnson worried rosary beads between her brown fingers. "Yeah, he wanted me to let mine grow out, so he could put it up."

I tried to flatten the springy curls that sprouted every which way from my skull. "Is Ricky's dad coming to see him soon?"

I knew from the nurses that Ricky's dad hadn't been at the hospital yet.

"No. He cannot come."

"Does he still hate Ricky for being queer? That's the stupidest—"

Bless her, she stopped me mid-rant. "No, it's not that. He feels horrible. He feels like this is his fault. He's ashamed."

"He better get over it! While he's wallowing in his mistake, Ricky is fighting for his life. It might help Ricky to have some sign of love from him." I knew it wasn't my place to lecture anyone's parents and butt my nose in private business, but Momma was at home with Allan and unavailable for the meddling and unsolicited advice. *I'm every bit my momma's daughter.*

Dr. Jonas came in. Short, stocky, his muscles strained against the fabric of his white coat as he held the chart in front of him and took command of the room. "Mrs. Johnson, Lorraine, it's good to see you both. Mrs. Johnson, in case you haven't heard about it, this young woman and her parents found Ricky and well, there's no other way to say it, they saved his life."

Mrs. Johnson chewed on her fist as she sobbed.

"Here's what I know. I will lower the dose on his pain medication over the next few days. I expect he will regain consciousness and we can begin feeding him through a straw. He's fought off infection. His wounds, although not completely healed, are at least closed. He had a fair amount of alcohol in his system and strangely, ketamine. I hope he will refrain from drug and alcohol use in the future." He continued perusing the flip chart.

"All systems are go! That's with the help of suppositories and we'll see how he does once he's conscious. If we can manage his pain, he could go home. His jaws are mending nicely, and the wires could come out in a week or so. I don't think there's any brain damage—no swelling, the scans are clear. Of course, we won't know some things until we can hear him talk and start walking, but I have reason to believe he'll be okay."

"Okay as anybody could be when someone tried to kill them," I said.

"You're right," Dr. Jonas said. "Ricky will need some help to get through the emotional trauma of this. Any word on taking the guy who did this off the street?"

"Not yet. Will Ricky need a nursing home?"

"I don't think so. He's young and strong. I think if we can get him off the tube and awake, he could start some rehab. Don't mistake what I'm saying. His care will be demanding, but I think it's better done by family." Dr. Jonas flipped the chart shut and rocked on his heels.

"That vet fellow, I saw him at the desk," Dr. Jonas began.

"Twitch is here? He's not on the visitor's list."

"I don't think he came in the room. He checked in with me, actually; and he said you'd probably like to take Ricky home to your place—what with his folks working out of the home." Dr. Jonas scanned Mrs. Johnson and then me. "Oh, how could I forget? Your mother, Mrs. Tyler, was here several times yesterday and today, stating in no uncertain terms that she wanted to care for him and wouldn't take no for an answer."

Mrs. Johnson gave a crooked smile and a barely perceivable nod.

"Is it okay if I bring Ricky home when he's ready?" I asked Ricky's mom. "I don't know if Momma would fight you for him, but she does seem like her mind's made up...please."

Mrs. Johnson smiled.

"You and your husband can come to our house any time to see him. You can stay overnight if you want...My momma's a great cook. She would feed you and we could play cards." I finally stopped my babbling when Maria hugged me again.

Chapter Seventeen

AFTER I LEFT the hospital room, I found Twitch pacing beside my truck in the hospital parking lot. He approached me as soon as he saw me. I hadn't worked with him or even seen him since the night Ricky got hurt and Twitch got wasted, bloody, and hateful about Ricky being himself at the bar.

"I know you probably aren't talking to me, but I have something to show you that might be important in figuring out who beat your friend."

"His name is Ricky."

"Ricky. Come on, Lorraine. Don't be like this. This is me, Twitch. I'm, I'm... Don't you remember who I am?"

"Did you have anything to do with Ricky getting hurt?" There. I'd said it. I'd been keeping myself from saying it, but I had thought it.

"What? You think I beat that boy?"

"I know you didn't think too much of him, your shirt was all torn, and it looked like dried blood on it. I saw it on the floor at your office."

Twitch stepped closer.

I stepped back.

"Lorraine, I didn't. I'd never do such a thing."

"How did your shirt get ripped? Whose blood was on it?" I cried even though I didn't want to.

"Oh, Lorraine." His shoulders slumped like maybe both Momma and I were standing on them. "My shirt was a mess because I was some place I shouldn't have been. Jack Allison came home early. Let's just say he was less than thrilled finding me visiting with Laura Allison. He grabbed me by my shirt and bloodied my nose. I'm embarrassed to tell you that, but relieved to tell you I didn't hurt Ricky and I never would."

Tears burned my eyes. I'd never spent any time hating Twitch before and it wasn't a comfortable occupation. "I'm sorry I thought what I thought. My brain is confused half the time. Of course, you wouldn't do that." I lowered my head. "I'm so tired." I cried like a teenage girl and blubbered my words. "Charity...we're done. Ricky and maybe me next. He had ketamine in him. School needs an answer. That creep at Grind's. I'm so tired."

Twitch touched my shoulder tentatively and I suppose since I didn't hit, kick, or bite him he hugged me. "It's going to be okay, Lorraine. Everything's going to be okay. Mumble and Shuffle will figure this thing out and then we can get back to normal."

I don't remember him hugging me since that day in the cemetery after Becky's burial when he and I talked for the first time since I found out he was our biological father. Momma had left home disgraced at eighteen. Her dad had accused her of whoring with Allister Grind and said her inattention to her younger brother had led to his accidental death in the corn bin. Momma had run off to Bend. A one-off encounter with Twitch had left her pregnant. She met Joseph a while later, fell in love, and married him knowing she carried his best friend's baby. Those facts made Momma, Dad, and Twitch the bravest people I ever met.

I leaned into his hug. It felt both good and foreign, probably to him too. He pulled away and fiddled with a clear plastic bag he took from his pocket. He quickly wiped a tear out of his eyes and dangled the bag in front of my face. "That broke off in a wound in Ricky's thigh. Your dad gave it to me."

Twitch silently watched as I examined the contents of the bag. The splinter was grayish white except where blood discolored it pinkish-brown. It could have been stone, or bone, or...*shit, I know what this is...where it's from and who...who freed it to use it as a weapon. Shit.*

"If I had my guess, I'd say that splintered-off whatever is what they used to stab and beat Ricky."

"Do you know what this is?" I asked.

"Yeah, I think I do. I wanted to get a second opinion from a good vet." He gave me a strained smile.

"It's horn, isn't it?"

"I think so. It doesn't prove anything. There's plenty of horns that get cut off, but it seems like a strange coincidence in my book."

"I guess fathers and daughters read a lot of the same books. What do we do now?"

"We don't do anything. I'm going to give this horn to Mumble and Shuffle. I think they will be interested in the evidence. I'll do a little investigation about where those horns ended up. Killer wasn't using them anymore, but somebody put them to use."

"The last time I saw them they were on the floor of the barn—*no, that's wrong.* I told Lewis to give them to McGerber and he'd know what to do with them. McGerber!"

"Shit, Lewis and Petey were at the Tavern the other night, but they were busy talking to Dr. Jacks and this guy I didn't recognize and a half-dozen college girls. I didn't talk to them."

"Lewis and Petey or the college girls?"

"Neither."

I took a balled-up paper out of my pocket and smoothed it out on the hood of my truck. "This is the list Kenny had constructed about who was at the tavern. Can you add anybody to it?"

Twitch traced his finger along each name on the roster. "I'm guessing Kenny meant Lewis and Petey when he wrote farmhands, but there could have been others. They were the only ones I recognized, but I didn't stay too close; they smelled like they live on a cattle ranch."

"Lewis and Petey had the horns. Do you think they would have—"

"No, I find that hard to believe. Do you think they would? How did they react to you?"

I remembered the day I first met them and the joke Lewis told about steers and queers. They'd seemed all right after that. We just got the work done. "They treated me okay."

"Ah hell, I guess we don't know for sure about anybody."

I told Twitch about the slick man at Grind's place and the articles Gerry had shown me.

"I can't say I'm surprised Grind joined up," Twitch said. "I find it a little farfetched that it's connected to what happened to Ricky."

"Well, if there is a connection, I better figure out who it is fast. I'm bringing Ricky home to our house when he's well enough."

"Be careful, Lorraine. It occurs to me and probably hasn't been lost on you that whoever did this may have some worries about getting found out. They might come back to eliminate the only witness."

The thought had already crisscrossed my mind a dozen times and now both Gerry and Twitch reminded me of the possibilities. *I'm in danger. If somebody in this town beat Ricky for being queer and he only lived here a short time, why wouldn't they come after the queer who's been here her whole life and doesn't go away?*

"I'll be fine."

Chapter Eighteen

TIME'S RUNNING OUT. Soon Ricky would be discharged from the hospital and be at our house and he still wouldn't be able to say who hurt him. How could I protect him if I didn't find out what happened? Mumble, Shuffle, and Sheriff Scrogrum were on the job, but they weren't about to give me any details on their investigation. I decided it was up to me to try to find the chain of custody on those horns I'd cut off McGerber's bull. I wasn't about to go to McGerber's to see if he still had them. I'd begin by tracking down Lewis and Petey.

Twitch had told me Lewis Gaus owned a tan-and-white kidney bean shaped camper. He parked it on whatever farm he and his friend, Petey Holman, worked. They called themselves the Winnebago Cowboys. I didn't know where they worked currently, but I had a pretty good idea where they would eat and drink when they had time off.

Late in the afternoon I stopped at the Lake Tavern. Miles from any sizable town, the Lake Tavern was an ideal drinking spot for lots of folks living in the country or vacationing in a rental cabin on the million lakes there were near Bend. The sand volleyball court baked in the sun on the west side of the voyager fort styled building, and a tarred parking lot could accommodate lots of cars and even some big truck rigs. The Lake Tavern sold cold beer in bottles and on tap, pull tabs, cigarettes, and the kitchen rolled out burgers, fries, onion rings, and homemade pizzas. What else did most people need?

When I arrived, the smells hit me. Kathy had just roasted chicken to perfection for the supper crowd and Doris washed beer glasses in bleach water. Doris's English accent could be heard over the country music playing on the jukebox. She told one of the summer folks to get their elbows off the table and another to wipe the ketchup and melted cheese from his face. I caught Doris and Kathy each separately and asked if they knew which farm Lewis and Petey worked. They didn't but agreed to ask the men to call me or call me themselves if they saw either man. They kept their promise when I returned from the bar bathroom.

"Lorraine, look what the cat dragged in." Kathy pointed at the door.

My stomach lurched and I took a quick intake of air. *This is getting real.* I hadn't thought about how I was going to approach the subject. Lewis and Petey sat at the bar drinking tap beer and buying pull tabs. I sat beside them. I had only been nervous when I drove there. I'd felt brave when I realized they weren't there. There was no way around but through, as my dad said. "You two were here the other night when Ricky got beat up."

"Hello to you too, Lorraine." Lewis craned his neck away from me. "Yeah, we were here, talked to Ricky some, talked to a lot of people."

"You have any idea who might have beat him up?" I asked.

Lewis turned his head and poked a finger into my shoulder. "If we would've seen who hurt that"—he hesitated and continued—"boy, don't you think we would've reported it to the sheriff?"

Petey didn't look at me. He concentrated on his beer.

My throat got tight. My voice squeaked. "I don't know. Would you? Did you see anything?" I hated being such a puke, but I truly didn't know who to trust. I'd already confronted Kenny and Twitch. I certainly had no loyalty to Lewis and Petey. Besides, it could be anybody...just like Gerry said. It was no accident that the KKK wore masks. Those groups weren't made up of otherworldly demons, they were made up of shopkeepers, bankers, farmers, teachers, and any other "normal folk" you could think of. They wore masks and robes to hide their identities and do their hateful things undercover.

"We were here, but we don't know who beat the kid up," Lewis said. "Anything else you want to ask us?"

"Just one other thing," I said. "What happened to the horns I cut off Killer the bull?"

"You told us to tell McGerber to shove them up his ass." Petey laughed. "Why?"

"Because I think one of them was used to stab Ricky."

Petey nearly knocked over his beer leaving the bar so quickly. He went out of the door. Lewis and I followed him to the parking lot where Petey had opened the driver's side door of Lewis's pickup truck. He rummaged under the seat.

"Shit, shit, shit!" Petey kicked in the gravel.

Lewis walked over and searched the same place Petey had looked. "Huh. They're gone." He went around to the other side of the truck and searched under the passenger seat. "God damn it, they were here, Lorraine. I didn't give 'em to old man McGerber because I thought they'd make good decorations in the Winnebago. Had them in the truck and never got around to putting them up in the trailer."

I remembered then that he had waved at me with them as we parted company the last day of drenching sheep at McGerber's farm.

"Maybe whoever moved the truck that night took them?" Lewis said.

"Somebody moved your truck?" I was confused.

"Yeah, it didn't make any sense. I thought maybe I forgot where I'd parked it, but I wasn't even that drunk. When we came out of the Tavern, my truck was on the other side of the lot."

"Who else has keys?" I asked.

Lewis frowned. "Oh, come on, Lorraine. Have you actually looked at my truck? Who in their right mind would steal it? Everyone knows I leave the keys in the ashtray. Hell, they might have still been in the ignition."

"Tell her about the seat," Petey said.

"Yeah, that's proof. Somebody shorter than me drove it because the seat was pulled up. Maybe that's when the car thief noticed the horns—when he was adjusting my seat."

It didn't make any sense to me. *It isn't when you pull up a seat that you notice what's underneath. It's when you put the seat farther back. From what Mumble and Shuffle deduced it was someone tall who last drove Ricky's car.* "What time did you notice the truck had been moved?"

"Well, I suppose since closing time is midnight it must have been about then." Lewis smiled.

He's lying. "I know the Tavern sometimes stays open a tad later than the official closing time. Are you sure about that time?"

Both Lewis and Petey blushed a bit.

We stood there avoiding eye contact for a beat.

"Lorraine, you got to know I wouldn't beat a kid up whether..." Lewis stopped talking.

"Whether what? Whether he was queer or not?" I asked.

Lewis's face reddened and Petey kicked at the dirt again, blushed, and gazed at the ground.

"Lorraine, don't make accusations you can't prove." Lewis glanced at Petey. Then he scanned the parking lot. A few of the people in the Tavern had filtered out, suddenly needing to check their tires or get something from their cars. Others didn't pretend to do anything other than watch us. He shook his head and squinted at me. "Just because you're some, I don't know, hot shot vet." He pulled off his cowboy hat and ran his fingers through his hair. He looked at the sky until he turned his scowl to me. "You pulled a part of a calf out of the ass of a cow. You don't know everything, Lorraine."

The way he said my name made me feel dirty.

"Come on, Petey."

Petey glanced at me like he had something to say, but then just got in the truck with Lewis.

Scared and mad at the same time I called to them, "Aren't you going to finish your beer?"

The two men drove away.

I called Twitch and left him a message that Lewis and Petey last had the horns on the night Ricky was hurt. They claimed they were stolen out of Lewis's unlocked vehicle. I didn't feel any closer to understanding what had happened or who did it. I felt like my pool of suspects was getting larger rather than smaller. *If Lewis and Petey were ever my allies, they aren't anymore.*

Chapter Nineteen

THE FOLLOWING SATURDAY while Momma, Dad, Kenny, and Allan went to the hospital to visit Ricky, I went to see a certain social worker on a horse ranch. No one questioned me about going, which was good because I would have lied at least a little. I would have explained that I needed to take a kitten to Addie. Certainly, delivering the kitten was important, especially because I said I would and Addie had helped save those kittens from McGerber's drowning scheme. *Why did I think up a lie? Charity is done with me. I can visit anyone I want.*

I wanted to know more about Marin England and I wanted to know something about myself. I wanted to know why I was both slack-jawed and infuriated during the same minute around her. I wanted to know how she could be so sure of herself and sure of me even though I had a girlfriend and I'd her told as much. *Wait, Lorraine. You haven't said shit about Charity to Marin. How did that sin of omission occur? Does it even matter now Charity avoids me?* Well, I could clear up my present romantic entanglement. *Whatever that is.*

The horse ranch was within our county. I'd driven by it a hundred times before and I knew the family had kids and horses, but I hadn't known the kids weren't there as part of a vacation or camp experience. I supposed these teens were like Addie—parents absent or unfit and no other family relations suitable or able to offer a home. I couldn't imagine not wanting my child or sending Allan to live at a place like this. Still, it seemed like an awfully pretty piece of land to call home. There were stands of trees dotted along the rolling hills. The pasture looked lush, some of it boggy and other parts had rocks heaving up from the ground like scabrous warts against the sea of green. A stream snaked through the land and in places cut through taller hills, giving the impression of a canyon with striated rock showing above the stream like layers of caramel, penuche, or fudge.

I didn't approach the white three-story farm house although I'd like to see inside. Both Marin and Addie were in the yard when I arrived. They sat at a picnic table with a group of other teenage girls of varying sizes and ethnicities. Addie got up from the table, ran over, and gave me a quick hug and said thanks for everything, but her attention zeroed in on the kitten I'd brought her. She took the gray tabby and nuzzled him under her chin.

"His name is Bugs, but you can change it if you want."

Addie smiled. "No, if you called him that, that's his name."

She looks well. Her clothes fit, she had color in her face, and she laughed and danced as she showed the kitten to the other girls.

Marin looks damn good. She hugged me too. Her hug seemed to last longer than Addie's. Marin whispered into my ear that I smelled nice which made me instantaneously blush and start sweating buckets.

"Thanks," I said. "You said something about me taking you out to lunch today."

"I'm way ahead of you. The more I thought about you coming out here, the more I thought I didn't want to share you with any restaurant. I made up a picnic basket for us."

Marin turned to where the girls crowded around Addie ogling her kitten and then looked back at me and winked. "Wait here with the girls while I saddle a couple horses for us."

I joined the girls at the table. Addie introduced me to everyone—Tandy, Vicki, LaQueesha, and Debbie. They didn't seem interested in me. They teased, pushed, and jostled one another. I couldn't follow half of what they were saying. I got that one of them received daily letters from a boyfriend and the other girls nagged her about it. When their own conversation flagged, I became an immediate source of inquiry and entertainment. Tandy, a redheaded girl about seventeen and six months pregnant, surveyed me like I might be for sale or applying for a job. "So, Lorraine, I understand you're here to teach the sex education class."

"Looks like I'm late for that," I said. *Smarty pants.* I wasn't afraid. I'd wrangled with my own sister plenty.

Tandy blushed.

The other girls laughed and high-fived one another.

"Are you a social worker?" LaQueesha asked me.

"God no! Not that there's anything wrong with social workers. I'm sure Marin's good. I'm studying to be a vet. I'm better with animals than people."

Tandy surfaced for more banter. "You should come back to the ranch tonight. We're having a pageant."

The other girls, including Addie, groaned.

"What's going on?" I asked.

"Oh, they're just mad because it's my turn to pick the Saturday night group activity and I picked a pretend beauty pageant," Tandy said.

"Yeah, and your beauty queen sash should read Miss Stick up her Ass," LaQueesha said.

"Or Missed Period," Debbie, a heavy-set dimple faced strawberry blonde girl, chimed in.

"Shut up, you fuckers. Tandy can't help she's pregnant. Her uncle raped her," Melody blurted out.

"Shut up, Melody. I don't want everybody knowing that," Tandy said.

A chorus of "sorrys" was followed by silence. Any playfulness we had evaporated quickly.

What was I supposed to say to that? "If you asked my momma, my sash would read Misaligned," I said. "If you asked my dad, it would read Mischievous. If you asked me, I'd write Misunderstood."

"We could all probably wear that sash," LaQueesha said.

"Misrepresented, misjudged. I could go on and on." I winked at Addie.

"Not me, call me Misdemeanor or Misadventure. I don't regret a damn thing I've done or blame anyone else for my life." Vicki was tall, brunette, and brassy. I hoped her bravado would get her through life.

Marin emerged from the barn. "Could one of you girls take one of these horses and somebody else take this picnic basket?" Vicki, Addie, and LaQueesha hustled over to help Marin. I couldn't take my eyes off the horses. They were beautiful and huge. I took the painted horse, the smaller of the two monsters. Marin mounted the black Appaloosa like it was nothing to lift her leg that high and nothing to muscle up onto the back of such a beast. It took all the flexibility I had to stretch up and get my foot in the stirrup and haul ass onto the saddle. Even then I nearly fell off the other side.

"You have ridden before, right?" Marin asked.

"Briefly. One time, Dad put me on a little too high on a horse. The horse lowered its head and I slid off the neck. Then he put me on again and the horse bucked me off on my butt. Does that count? Oh, and I should mention it was a Shetland pony. These horses probably shit bigger than that horse."

To her credit, Marin smiled, but she didn't laugh at me—the girls did. Thankfully, Marin didn't cancel the whole excursion.

"Sorry, girls, I think you're going to have to put these two back." She stuck out her lower lip and then smiled. "Desperate times call for desperate measures. Bring us Herc." Marin dismounted. I did the same, but not as gracefully. I thought I might have jammed my legs into my armpits jumping down from that height.

"What's a Herc?" I asked.

"It's short for Hercules. He's a big quarter horse, strong, fast, but retired from racing. He can carry the both of us without any difficulty." Then she leaned in and whispered, "You are okay if we have to ride seated really close together?"

"No, I don't mind." I'm sure I looked scared shitless, but it had only a little to do with the giant horse. I couldn't have mounted Herc myself without a pole vaulting maneuver. Luckily, Addie and one of the other girls brought a small stepladder over for me. They giggled the whole time as I climbed and crawled onto the monster.

Marin didn't need the ladder. She stretched up as far as she could, grasped the saddle horn, put her foot in the stirrup, hoisted herself on top of the horse, and snugged up behind me. She put her arms around me and took the reins. As she enveloped me in her arms, the seams of my jeans rode up against me and I was pressed against the saddle horn. I remembered what Ricky said about horse riding being good foreplay. I worried that if we rode very far my underwear would be permanently lodged up my netherlands or my eyes would roll back in my head.

The girls divided the picnic basket between the pouches of the saddle bags, opened the gate to the pasture, and waved to us. Marin said everyone else at the ranch was going to St. Wendell to a matinee. She said it was rare to have the ranch to ourselves. I wondered how that rare occurrence took place on the very day Marin asked me to come over. My face flushed at my audacity. *She's probably just being nice inviting me here. She probably doesn't want to get in trouble for exposing impressionable girls to the town lesbian.* Then again, I didn't believe in coincidences.

"I hope you don't mind my face so close to yours. I like the way my head fits over your shoulder. It gives me a clear view of the trail and I can smell that light perfume you wear."

"It's just my shampoo." *Dumb, dumb, dumb!* She was flirting with me and I didn't recognize it.

The motion of the horse was mesmerizing, but Marin's voice so close to my ear and neck made my eyes cross. The hairs stood up on my neck, my arms broke out in goose bumps and my nipples were at attention. Christ, how long had it been since I was with Charity? I couldn't remember. That wasn't true. It had been four and a half weeks since I'd seen her. It had been six weeks since we had been together to even kiss or nuzzle. We hadn't been together-together for nine weeks. By my estimate that was seven wasted years in lesbian time.

Marin told me more about the ranch, how a friend of hers from graduate school, another social worker, owned it. This friend gravitated to the treatment of trauma end of services. I wondered if Marin had any other connections to this person but didn't chance asking.

"The kids pick up a work ethic from performing the chores on the ranch, but they're caring for animals that have never hurt them or betrayed them," Marin said. "The animals give back and the girls can decide what they want to take in."

"Too bad the kids can't be with their families, though." I said it like I knew something about it.

"Is it? I know for me, getting away from my family ended up a good thing. Not every family is like yours, Lorraine."

"That's a relief."

"Oh, come on, are you telling me you have it rough?"

"Well, my momma keeps bringing home bachelors for me to meet and hopefully marry. She knows I'm queer and I..." I started to say Momma knew I had a girlfriend, but I stopped myself. *Why did I stop myself?* "She knows I'm queer and I don't need a boyfriend."

"Well, we have being queer and not needing a boyfriend in common, Lorraine." Marin squeezed me in her arms as she held the reins.

As we rode across the flat pasture Marin told me she too grew up out of her parents' home. "My mom never intended harm or danger. She meant well, but after my dad died, when I was six, she couldn't pick a boyfriend to save her life. She picked a few who could've ended both our lives. The worst one, Doug, drove drunk and hit a truck. Both he and my mom were killed. My first foster placement happened at age fifteen."

"I'm sorry, Marin."

The landscape changed from flat pasture to rolling hills with stands of pine and mixes of oak, maple, and birch trees. The leaves of the trees danced in the breeze and shone silver against a cloudless blue hydrangea sky. Marin prodded Hercules into a gallop, but the horse had no trouble carrying us. On the way up the hills, I leaned back into Marin and on the way down, she pressed against me. I couldn't tell you a single name of a flower or bird I saw although I'd bet there were plenty, but I could tell you exactly every place on my skin that her hands touched me, the way her arms felt as they blanketed my own, and every place her breasts pressed against my back. It was all I could do not to turn around and kiss her.

"Here's the spot I wanted you to see," she said.

She pointed to the part of the creek I'd noticed from the road. Here the waterway narrowed to not more than twelve feet across and snaked through a small valley bending and straightening between thin sandy banks, swaying grasses, and wildflowers in blues, yellows, purple. Outcroppings of rocks and groups of trees lined the stream bed, but left a circle of bare ground, flat, partially shaded, like someone had recreated a museum painting of a picnic scene.

Marin dismounted and put her arms out to me. "Throw your leg over, I'll catch you."

I did as she said, my eyes glued to hers. I slid off the horse and fell toward the earth. My legs, then my thighs and hips slid through her hands, but she caught me at the waist and pulled me against her. We were face to face. My feet were off the ground and my head was somewhere in the clouds.

"Lorraine, you fit so nicely in my arms and hands." She lowered me to the ground. I had sea legs. I staggered and my insides turned all gooey.

"Are you flirting with me, Marin?"

"Wow, I thought I was being pretty obvious."

"Well, I didn't want to presume, and I didn't know if you knew about Charity, my girlfriend, kinda."

"Yeah, I know. I also know she has been away a lot. Long-distance relationships are tough. Maybe you're broken up?"

"How do you know stuff about me?"

"I have a confession to make. I know a lot about you because we have a mutual friend. Gerry Narrows is my aunt."

"Well, I'm relieved you know Gerry and it isn't because you have some file about me. You don't have a file about me, do you?"

"Just in my head. No. I don't have a file on you, but when I wrote Gerry I would be working here in Jewitt County, she thought I might want to meet her friend, Lorraine. I also admit after I met you, I asked Gerry whether you were seeing anyone. She told me she wasn't sure and maybe there had been some changes in circumstances with you and Charity. Do you want to know what Gerry told me specifically about you?"

I nodded.

"She said you were kind, compassionate, smart, and a hard worker. All those traits are attractive to me. Then I saw how pretty you were. Well, I found myself smitten. If I may use such an old-fashioned expression."

What are the names of shades of red and pink? I'm guessing all of them passed across my face. I felt like Rudolph when Clarice said he was cute and he jumped and impressed the other reindeer with his flying skills. But I worried something glaring about me would spoil the whole thing, like when Rudolph's fake nose fell off.

Before any body parts fell off or I said anything dumb, Marin cupped my cheek in her hand and kissed me. Her kiss was soft and chaste. "I'll get the picnic food. I have some bottles of pop cooling in the stream in a fish net. Will you find them for us?" She pointed to a section of water.

Drinks cooling in a stream, how romantic is that? That wasn't all. While I retrieved the drinks, Marin laid out a red-and-white gingham checked blanket and a picnic spread of fried chicken, potato salad with black and green olives, and sliced watermelon. And she used cloth napkins. I felt like I'd fallen into the pages of a romance novel.

"You planned all this for me?"

"For us." She lay back on the picnic blanket, laced her fingers together behind her head, and gazed up at me. "Lorraine, I believe in romance. I believe in all the little sweet things a person can do to make somebody feel special." She sat up again. "But don't get the idea I do this for lots of people. I only risk the sweet things on the sweet. I only lavish my attentions on someone I'm ready to care about in a big way and whom I trust has the capacity to do the same for me."

Marin leaned in and kissed me. "Lorraine, I think you are sweet, kind, funny, incredibly sexy, and I am willing to take a risk on you even if you aren't free to return my trust. For now, let me be sweet to you and let's just have fun."

Gulp. I could sure use some sweetness and fun. I didn't feel guilty. Granted, we didn't kiss any more that afternoon. We laughed. God, I can't remember when I had laughed so hard, certainly not any time recent. I had expected lots of hard luck stories that would make me weep. Again, I was wrong. She told stories about her time in college at a state school known for partying more than scholarship. She told me her coming out story, her crushes and one three-year relationship that had ended a year ago, but she still had some residual emotional bruising. I told her about dehorning Killer, but the story made us laugh. I felt no anger or disgust for McGerber. I had survived and had a good story to tell from the experience. It was a win.

After lunch had settled Marin and I packed up our picnic—the things we had brought with us and the preinstalled romantic trimmings. She helped me onto Herc again. The horse seemed shorter to me. Marin put her arms around me and held the reins. I settled into her more than I had on the way there. During our mutual story telling I hadn't said much about Charity. It felt too private, but I thought I could talk to her now and maybe understand something better myself.

"I have been trying to write a letter to Charity, but I can't seem to finish it."

"Oh, what is it you want to say?"

"It's more what I want to ask. I feel like I need to ask her if we broke up and I don't even know about it."

"Well, it doesn't sound like a 'we' thing. Sounds like she hasn't been communicating with you as you would appreciate and expect if you're partners together. Charity's not the only voice in the discussion."

"Maybe I already know the answer. Maybe I've had trouble asking the question because leaving it like it is means I don't have to deal with us being over."

"Maybe."

"You know that Charity's sister, Jolene, was in my class and my best friend. I had a baby crush on her for years. That was before I knew there was anybody in the world like me. Jolene is incredible, but she's not queer. Then, I met Charity—she was so beautiful and assertive and queer—and she liked me. It seemed like the most natural thing in the world to get together. When we kissed, pardon me if this is too much information, but when Charity and I kissed I felt like all the fears I had about being the only queer in the world went away and I had a future with love and fun."

"That's not weird to say. It makes perfect sense."

"I didn't have a clue. Then when we made love, it seemed like we were together, and I liked it and figured that's how we'd be, forever."

"Yeah, I hear you. Where are queer women supposed to practice dating when it isn't accepted to be gay? We take our patterns from the straight world, but it doesn't fit so easily when your sexuality isn't an accepted thing. Your sister could openly date the man she married and decide comparing him to millions of other men and examples of straight relationships in the world."

"Becky did have choices I guess. They had to hide their making-out, but only because they were young and not married yet. They could at least date in the open."

"There are jokes about lesbians moving fast into long-term relationships, but it's true and it's logical. Probably most or at least many women are interested in relationships not just sexual encounters. But without having an open way to meet other lesbian women it seems kind of natural that a woman might partner up with the first person she meets who also loves women."

"Add to that the horndog factor."

She squeezed me tighter. "Yep, there's definitely that. If you're brought up to believe you only have sex with your marriage partner, it's natural you might see yourself as married to Charity. It seems to me marriage should be more of a conscious choice than that. Say a person impulsively has sex with someone, should those two automatically be considered married? Kenny and Becky had sex before marriage. Did that make them automatically married?"

"No, but once Becky got pregnant there was a big push to get them married as fast as possible."

"Sometimes that works out okay I guess, but I think it's a mistake for people to get married just based on a sexual experience with each other. There needs to be more time and more knowing each other."

I didn't say any more. I didn't ask Marin if we were in that getting to know each other more time or if we were dating. I didn't promise to finish my letter to Charity. I just rode along on the big horse with Marin's arms around me, and I felt like I didn't have a care in the world and I wished we could just keep riding.

WHEN WE RETURNED from the picnic it surprised me that Addie sat alone at a picnic table. She appeared sad or angry or maybe both. While Marin stabled the horses, I went to talk with Addie.

"Hey, I thought you were going to a movie?" I planned to sit down by Addie, but she abruptly got up.

Before she walked away she screamed at her phone. Then she shot me a look. "Why do we bother to love anyone? They all just use us or judge us and leave us. Men are nothing but dangerous liars. I wish I could be a queer like you and Ricky." She stormed off toward the house.

I didn't know if Marin caught any of that, but I didn't wait to find out. I got in my truck and drove home. *Who is Addie mad at? She sounded like she had a small crush on Ricky that day at the farm, but now she knows he's gay. Where's Addie getting her information?*

Chapter Twenty

FINALLY, ENOUGH DAYS passed, and Ricky had recovered enough to come home to our farm. He'd passed the discharge test. He could get up and walk to the bathroom without assistance. Momma cooked up a storm as soon as she got the word he was coming home. She made all his favorite recipes—a pointless exercise since he could only eat pureed foods. She set herself up in my old room downstairs so she'd be close by and she made a place for Ricky in the living room complete with a nest on the couch. Grandma's quilt, an incense diffuser, magazines, a TV with remote—that was a waste, we still got only two channels—a boom box with all of Momma's favorite CDs in jeweled cases, and a table close by with everything within reach. Just to be safe she bought what she called a nifty nabber so he could grab something from farther away. That is, he could nifty nab once his broken fingers healed.

He didn't even laugh about the nifty nabber. It didn't feel like he was home. For one thing, he still couldn't talk and Ricky loved to talk. He couldn't talk or smile his impish grin or offer advice on my appearance. He wasn't himself. He slept most of the time or seemed dopey on heavy-duty painkillers. His mouth still looked like he tried to swallow a shopping cart—his jaw wired shut.

I helped him eat by squirting syringes of water and nutritional shakes through a gap in his teeth. He seemed to lose weight daily. His mouth and the areas around his eyes weren't as swollen, but his hands were puffy paddles. His purple bruises had faded to greenish yellow.

I expected Ricky to tell me what had happened that night as soon as he was able. To me, he seemed able. He could talk enough to tell us which flavor of gruel he wanted. His fingers were broken and splinted, but his neck wasn't. I thought he'd at least answer yes and no questions and help the sheriff, Mumble, and Shuffle to bring the bastards to justice, but when I asked him stuff he didn't answer me or nod or shake his head in the right places. He just closed his eyes and waved me off like he couldn't remember.

I wanted to show him mug shots and ask him to nod if he saw the bastards who beat him, not that I had any mug shots. I did have some high school yearbooks, a church directory, and some newspaper clippings of local softball leagues.

A mime by day, at night Ricky had night terrors—he wrestled and defeated his sheets and blankets from the bed. His muffled screams and his crying awakened everybody in the house except Allan. I went downstairs to him.

His eyes were wide and at first, he pushed me away, but then he let me hold him and rock him. "I've got you, Ricky. You're safe." His eyes peered into mine like he didn't recognize me. It took a long time before his breathing slowed, and his eyes darted around like he'd never feel safe even in our house, even in my arms. *My God. What did they do to you?* Eventually, he was too exhausted to keep watch. He relaxed in my arms and fell asleep.

I had heard about post-traumatic stress disorder from daytime talk shows and prime time dramas. It didn't surprise me that it was painful for Ricky to think about the beating and thinking it was akin to reliving it. *I get it.* I had watched my sister stab herself and drop into fire. I knew PTSD intimately. I just thought the need to expose the beaters would outweigh the fears. Of course, I didn't have a tangible person to blame for Becky's death other than myself.

Mumble and Shuffle called it a hate crime and said similar things had happened in other places. It wasn't that I didn't know, but I'd refused to think about people in my own community taking it upon themselves to punish queers. I thought the job had been given and wrongly attributed to some people's gods. Maybe it was now contracted out to less expensive venders.

I tucked Ricky into his nest. I mostly yammered on about something from *People* magazine or something cute Allan had done, but all the time I found myself impatient wondering when and if Ricky was going to tell us who hurt him. Was he protecting us?

"Good night, Ricky. See you in the morning. I better get out to the kitchen. Sounds like Dad is searching out Momma's new hiding spot for his beer." I kissed him quick on the top of the head, turned on the night light Momma got him, and went into the kitchen to join Dad.

"He can't sleep." Dad had a tall glass of milk in front of him. He massaged his feet through his socks. Dad's double-barreled shotgun and a box of shells were on the chair next to him.

"I don't know if he'll ever sleep. I don't know if he'll ever tell anyone who did this." I poured a glass of water from the pitcher in the fridge, but my eyes were glued to that gun. Dad kept his guns in a safe and never left his guns and ammunition in the same spot unless he was planning to go hunting.

"Snitches get stitches—isn't that what they say?" Dad lowered his head as he glanced at me. "Maybe he's afraid there's more coming. Maybe he thinks he's protecting himself and all the rest of us."

"Is that why you got that gun out, Dad? You want us to take up arms?"

"No, Lorraine, I don't want you to take up arms, but it occurs to me that Ricky isn't safe and by extension this family isn't safe."

"So, what, you going to guard us?"

"I just thought it might make sense to be ready if some ruffians come to the house to hurt Ricky." He played it off like it was a joke, but I knew full well Dad wouldn't have a loaded gun in the house unless he couldn't come up with another way to keep us safe.

"Be ready? Be ready to shoot somebody, Dad?"

"I don't know, Lorraine." He picked up the gun and placed it on the table between us. "I want to protect my family."

"With a loaded gun? For how long, Dad? How long are you going to be keeping watch over this family? That's about as dumb an idea as Ricky thinking that not telling on the pukes who beat him will keep them from finishing the job." I stood up and poured my water out in the sink.

This is getting out of hand. "If that's Ricky's logic, it's stupid logic. It's an illusion of control. You can't stop bad things from happening by ignoring them or not telling about them. It's the telling about bad behavior that gets people thinking about it and demanding change. For those who can't stop hurting people, they need to be separated from people to hurt. And regular people like us taking up arms isn't sustainable and it isn't safe. We're more likely to shoot each other than any ruffian."

"Maybe neither me nor Ricky are as hopeful as you are that whoever did this will be held accountable." Dad opened the box of shells and removed two. "I'm just going to load it and hide it behind that big armchair in the living room across from Ricky's spot. Allan can't get at it, but you and I will both know where it is and I'll let Kenny know too."

"You going to let Momma know?"

He didn't say anything.

"I didn't think so."

Dad was right that we were in danger. Whoever'd hurt Ricky could and would probably hurt him or somebody else again because the hurting wasn't connected to the telling. Its tendrils attached to the hating and feeling powerful by hurting someone else. I didn't agree with his decision to have a loaded gun in the house, but I decided I'd argue that stupid logic another day. I just nodded at him as he loaded the shotgun. Then I left Dad sitting at the table and went back into the living room, where I was certain Ricky was not yet asleep.

"If you think not telling's going to keep you safe, you're wrong. The asshole who did this is still out there and maybe next time he'll take a few other queers or their family with him." I hated playing the card that he was protecting someone who might hurt me and mine, but desperate times called for ingenuity not loaded guns. I had to get him to talk and put this whole thing to rest.

He did that closing his eyes and turning away from me thing he usually did.

"Don't you dare ignore me. I've been here for you. Christ knows our whole family has been here for you." I saw tears in the corners of his eyes, his nose ran, but he didn't wave me off. Watching him cry made me feel like a bully. Chipmunk Ricky, pretty boy with the delicate bones of a bird. *How could anyone smash a chipmunk?* I backed off, but only a bit.

"You have a doctor's appointment tomorrow. Then we'll know when the wires come out of your jaw. The day it happens, you better be ready to talk. Do you understand me?"

He opened his eyes, looked at me, and nodded.

"Good. I'm glad we've got that settled. Nobody else needs to get hurt. It's going to be okay, Ricky. I promise."

I went to my room and cried. *I lied to him. I don't know if it will ever be okay again.*

THE NEXT DAY Ricky met with the doctor. Momma, Dad, and I were all there with Ricky. Dr. Jonah said he would remove Ricky's wires the following Thursday. I had felt like celebrating. I announced probably too freely and too loudly it would be the day Ricky would tell me who hurt him. The last Thursday of the month loomed large. The sheriff, Mumble, and Shuffle said they'd be at our house with their questions and a tape recorder. Momma, Dad, Kenny, and Twitch wanted to be there. I had expected Russ would want to hear, but he hadn't even visited Ricky. I heard Pastor Grind announced in church that the vengeance of God had been taken out against a young sinner whom he planned to visit and bring to repentance. So, probably just about everybody knew Ricky was ready to name his attacker. If the culprit remained in town, he likely heard he had a deadline to leave or finish what he'd started.

Perhaps I could legally change my name to Idiot or Screw Up. I'd made so many mistakes, hurt Ricky's feelings, and maybe put him in more danger. Plus, there was now a loaded shotgun in a makeshift cardboard holster velcroed to the back of the fuzzy armchair in the living room. As if that wasn't enough to worry about, Charity came back to town without telling me she was coming, and she stopped at the farm the day after Ricky met with the doctor and I had heralded his disclosure date to the world.

The dogs went nuts when they got Charity's scent. I knew the feeling. They had missed her too. I watched from the window as she gave attention to each dog—rubbing their bellies and scratching their ears. Her hair was longer and her face was more tanned, but her freckles showed. God, she was wearing jeans, a lacy tank top tucked in at the waist so I couldn't help but notice that perfect waist and those long legs.

"Ricky, Charity is here. I'm going to go talk with her outside on the porch. Keep an eye on Little Man, I mean Allan. Allan, you watch over Ricky. Maybe paint his toenails. There's polish in Ricky's beauty kit." I pointed the large burgundy tackle box that housed Ricky's tools of the cosmetology trade. I left Ricky in his nest in the living room. If Ricky had any objections he couldn't say, and I didn't care. I checked on the clandestine shotgun and made certain Allan couldn't see or reach it. I just wanted at least a few minutes alone with Charity.

She hugged me when I came out on the porch. Her hand cuffed the back of my neck and we stood there quiet for what seemed like a long time. It was a hug you give someone when they are hurt or grieving. I wondered which or if both of us were about to know more loss. She kissed me lightly on the lips, but there was no urgency or hint of need from either of us. We sat on the front porch swing together, both of us staring out into the yard instead of at each other.

"I didn't know you were coming. It's good to see you. I've been trying to write a letter to you. It's taking me the longest time to finish it." I examined my hands. I have Momma's hands—small hands, thumbs like spoons—shit for texting. They would normally be on some part of Charity. Why were they just there in my lap, unemployed?

"Sorry, I didn't call and tell you I was coming. My mom said you would likely be around because you were helping your mom nurse Ricky. How's he doing?"

"He's mending, but he still won't tell us who did it. I don't get why he won't say it."

"Maybe it was someone he knew who hurt him, and it's hard to name someone who would betray him. It's hard to admit people we love hurt us."

Ah, crap! Is it me or is she speaking code for us? "I was right. We are broken up." That was brave of me considering I didn't want to know the answer.

"Oh, Lorraine, I think...I hoped you'd just lose interest in me or be mad and tell me off. You're just so...loyal."

"You make it sound like a bad thing—being loyal." I wouldn't apologize for one of my best traits. *Well, it is one of my best traits if I ignore that I just kissed Marin.*

Charity leaned into me. "I didn't mean this to happen."

"What has happened exactly?"

"I have a chance to go to Europe. It's an art tour through Italy, France, and Spain. I can visit museums and churches. I can paint in the open air where artists have painted for centuries."

"That's great! I'm so happy for you." I hugged her. "How did this happen? Did you get a grant? Wait, you make it sound like this trip is the reason we can't be together. I've always supported your art."

"In order to properly take advantage of this opportunity I would need to be gone a year for sure and probably two."

Something sounded scripted about the way she talked.

"I'm going with Kelly."

Shit.

"I'm thinking about getting back together with Kelly."

Thinking about...that's a whole trailer load of shit! Now I know the playwright who scripted Charity's message.

"I'm sorry, Lorraine, but I know myself and there's probably no way I won't *be* with her if we travel like that together for more than a year. It feels inevitable."

I squinted at her wondering if she had become possessed.

"Lorraine, to be fair I've been thinking of calling it off with you, but I wasn't sure and didn't know how to tell you."

My throat felt swollen shut. I couldn't speak. I swallowed and nodded, looked at my small, strong hands. *Tell her, you coward. I've been writing you a breakup letter. I already know it's over. I kissed Marin. She's sweet on me...* I didn't say anything.

"Lorraine, I don't want to live in Bend. I think you would be fine living here, but I know I wouldn't. Eventually, we'd be at this point and I know I couldn't stay here and this is where you said you want to be even after you finish veterinary school. This was inevitable, Lorraine."

There was that word again, "inevitable."

"I can't believe you decided for me. Maybe it was inevitable, but I'd have liked to have been a part of the decision."

"Well, are you saying you're willing to accept that I'm with Kelly and will be traveling with her for a year or more? Are you saying you want to wait for me and see if we can be together after all this?"

I looked at her. Beautiful, beautiful Charity! My first true love. My first and only lover. Could I wait for her while she traveled with Kelly, loving Kelly? I looked at myself, loyal and true; my hands, small, strong, skilled, and empty.

Charity must have been uncomfortable with the silence. She retreated a bit in her decision. "I don't know, Lorraine. Maybe we can stay together and make it through this. I know I can't promise I won't be with Kelly sexually because I would be lying. Let me think more about this and I'll call you."

What were we supposed to do next? I don't suppose she knew any better than I did, although she'd had more experience with breakups than I did. She'd broken up with Kelly and she'd broken up with me before. We stood up, faced each other. We hugged. We both cried. We stayed like that for I don't know how long. Then we let go. Charity left.

Chapter Twenty-One

MOMMA CAME HOME just about the time I'd removed the nail polish Allan had painted on Ricky's toes, feet, and up his legs. I put a blanket over the polish that landed on the arm of the couch.

"Lorraine, you would not believe the day I have had. If Doctor Jacks doesn't leave Bend I may have to kill him myself."

"Kill him myself," Allan echoed.

I must admit I wasn't listening, but Ricky seemed attentive and Allan was there so Momma kept talking.

"Would you believe he smelled of alcohol when he came to the clinic today?"

"Stinky," Allan said.

"That's right it's stinky and a man of medicine has no business showing up at his place of work impaired by chemicals. And he smokes."

Ricky mustered some animation for Momma's tale. He shook his head, agreeing with Momma. I guessed that meant improvement since he was sucking up to Momma.

"I confronted him, and you know what he said?"

I had no idea, but I knew she was going to tell me and whatever he said pissed her off more.

"He said I was a fat, controlling, self-righteous woman."

"Fat contwirling," Allan said.

I could have bet Ricky was glad his jaws were wired shut, and he had no obligation to say anything to Momma. It fell on me and I didn't exactly disagree with Dr. Jacks. Still, I didn't like him hurting my family and he hadn't lived in Bend long enough to insult and offer critical feedback to my momma.

"I'm sorry, Momma. That was a nasty thing for him to say." What else was I supposed to say? My plate was full. "I hope your pain gets better and you don't kill him. There's no room in this house for killing or killers."

Then I asked Momma to keep watch over Ricky and Allan for me. I got out of the house and drove my truck without the thought of a destination.

DRIVING HAD ALWAYS cleared my head or at least given me the privacy to cry. I wanted a distraction. I didn't want to think of Momma and her fight with Dr. Jacks, Charity, or Ricky, Little Man—Allan, Allan, Allan...or my stalled education, or my future as a vet or a girl lover. I wanted to watch a movie or a game. I wanted to be a spectator and not an actor in something for a while. *Everything changes. Momma usually tells me what to do or think. I can't think what to do or how to help.* Without remembering or intending to drive there, I found myself at the Lake Tavern. I parked, went inside, and ordered a Coke. I had only been there a few minutes when Petey and Lewis arrived.

If they were tentative about talking to me after the grilling I'd given them the last time we spoke, they didn't show it. I had shivers and it took some concentration not to shake in my boots or run for the bathroom. There were a couple of glances exchanged between us. I nodded.

Lewis nodded. Petey came over to me and Lewis followed with the familiar swagger I noticed at the McGerber farm. He didn't smile, but he didn't spit tobacco at my shoes either.

Lewis nudged Petey.

"I remembered something," Petey said.

"Oh? What's that?"

"I remembered I lied," Petey said. "And I lied to both of you."

"What are you talking about?" Lewis said. "You never told me about any lie."

"I know and I'm sorry," Petey said. "I'm telling you now."

He appeared all hangdog like he'd messed the house and his pitiful mutt mug might save him from a scolding.

"I showed those horns to some boys that night and I'm the one who moved the truck."

"What? Why?" Lewis socked Petey in the shoulder. "You dumb ass!"

"Ouch!" Petey winced.

"What boys?" I asked. I didn't care if Petey drove that truck in the Rose Parade. I was interested in who might have hurt Ricky.

"There were some college boys here that night, the night Ricky was hurt," Lewis said. "Now it sounds like Petey here showed them the horns and moved my truck."

"Those blonde girls were hanging all over those boys and so impressed with their football letters and all that crap," Petey said. "You were talking to them too, Lewis, like they were so interesting. I got those boys' attention and asked if they ever saw horns from a killer bull? They would've seen me put them back under the truck seat. Maybe they took them."

"Where was I during all this?" Lewis cuffed Petey in the side of the head.

"I don't know. In the bathroom or talking to those guys by the pool table." Petey rubbed his head where Lewis had hit him.

"Who were these guys, Lewis? Petey, were they with anyone you recognized?" *Finally, I was getting closer to some suspects.*

"I don't know who they were. They wore letterman jackets—St. Luke's, I think. I saw them talking and laughing with Ricky before."

"Did you catch any of their names? Would you recognize them if you saw them again, Petey?"

"Maybe, they had little gold footballs on their jackets. I suppose they're on St. Luke's football team, but I don't know what year."

"Ricky had mentioned there was an older man who seemed interested in him." *Damn if I wasn't on a roll. Look out, Mumble and Shuffle. Almost-a-vet is a crime solving machine.*

"I don't know who that could be." Lewis glanced at Petey.

Petey shook his head.

"Kenny said you were talking to an older guy he didn't know."

"Oh, Warren? He's harmless," Lewis grinned. "We gave McGerber's brother some razzing is all."

"What were you giving him shit about?" I remembered McGerber had been primping for his brother's visit the days I worked at his farm with Lewis and Petey.

"Oh, when he's sober he's all—save America from evil, communism, blah, blah, but once he starts drinking he's probably still a patriot, but he's no saint. He's pointing out which women he wants to know biblically if you get my meaning," Lewis wiggled his eyebrows. "He was going on about how he was about to have a big pay day, but the leech kept bumming cigarettes from me."

"Did he mention the Traditional Party?"

"That might have been it," Lewis looked away. "It's above my pay grade." Then Lewis turned to Petey. "I still don't know why you lied to me about moving the truck?"

"You told me not to, but I went to see Addie, but she was gone," Petey said.

"Addie!" I stepped closer to Petey. "You're Addie's boyfriend? You got her pregnant?" I wanted to punch the fool.

"I'm sorry, but I love Addie." Petey got all hangdog again. He swayed side to side as he spoke. Then he perked up. "What did you just say, Lorraine?"

"Shit." Lewis took off his cowboy hat. "Addie is pregnant? You dumb ass, Petey."

"Don't worry, she's not pregnant anymore." I regretted the words as soon as they were out of my mouth. "She had a miscarriage." So much for subtly and sensitivity. *I have the bedside manner of Dr. Jacks.*

Petey turned a greenish yellow like he would pass out.

Lewis put his arm around Petey. "I'm sorry, Pete. That's a sad thing," he said flatly.

Petey was likely in shock. I imagine any guilt he felt about his lying was eaten up by the sadness he felt for Addie and that baby. For a while I forgot that dumb ass had sex with a sixteen-year-old. It was legal, but it wasn't right. I was glad he didn't know where she was even if he seemed to feel bad about the baby.

Lewis turned to me. "Here's what we're going to do. We're going to stake out the Tavern, watch for those boys. Here, give me your cell phone and I'll put my number in visa versa." He took my phone. "Once we find them, we'll tie them up for you and the sheriff."

"Thanks, I guess." I didn't know what I'd do with them if Lewis and Petey hog-tied a group of boys for me. I knew I couldn't stay at the Tavern any longer. I was still digesting that Petey and Addie had been together. It was no respite to anything.

Petey took me by the shoulders and turned me toward him. "Lorraine, thanks for telling me about Addie. I'm sorry I didn't tell you about those college guys before."

"Here's your phone, Lorraine." Lewis handed it back to me.

My head was swimming. "Call me when you see those boys." *It really wasn't McGerber who impregnated Addie.* "Petey, Addie is getting on with her life. She's been through a lot. Maybe you oughta find someone your own age."

Chapter Twenty-Two

I DROVE NORTH, away from our farm, the Lake Tavern, Bend, and everything familiar. I tried to make sense of what had happened over the last few days. I listed the chaos out loud in the truck. "Charity's going to Europe with Kelly, Marin declared she's sweet on me, and Ricky's about to name his attackers. Shit."

I wish I could go into a medically induced coma. I wouldn't have to think about any of it. I was tired and sickened. The truth of what hurt people could put on one another rattled around in my head. *Brutes beat a sweet boy like Ricky and leave him for dead just because he's gay. Grown men have sex with teenagers. Haters are elected officials and have a taxpayer paid forum to spew hate and make it into policy. The church sometimes feels obliged to sponsor the haters or vice versa.* Tears ran down my face. I had to pull over to wipe my eyes, so I could see to drive. At least it was still daylight. I didn't need to be as vigilant for deer as I would at dusk in a half hour or so.

My cell phone rang. *Shit. I'm not answering. It's probably Momma.*

The phone kept ringing. *Maybe it's an emergency with Allan or Ricky.*

I answered the phone.

"We got them—well, two of them!"

"What?"

"It's me, Petey. I'm calling to tell you we got those two college boys and guess who pulled into the parking lot right after they did?"

"I don't know." Then it sounded like he dropped his phone. "Petey."

"Ouch." Petey came back on the phone. "Lewis said he'll tell you when he sees you."

I pulled my truck onto the shoulder of the road. "Petey, tell me who else was involved with this."

"Can't. Don't worry, Lorraine. Lewis gave him a tongue lashing about how much trouble he's in when Ricky's wires come off tomorrow. He drove off and Lewis left after him."

"What are the college guys saying, Petey?"

"Lorraine, your phone is breaking up," Petey said. "Lewis and I will meet you at your house. Ricky is going to be surprised about us getting those boys. Don't tell him until we get there with that other fool."

"Any idea where the guy Lewis is chasing was headed?"

"I don't know, but he high-tailed it out of here and took off in a big shiny black truck. Hey, that preacher Grind and old man McGerber came through all frantic and serious. They were asking if anybody out at the Lake Tavern had seen you. I told them they should go home and lock their doors. There's some outlaw faction of that Traditional Party creeping around town."

Great! "Where'd Grind and McGerber go?" I asked.

"They all headed west toward town or your place I guess," Petey said. "Didn't they get there yet?"

"I'm not home."

"Where are you now?"

"Just about twenty minutes from our farm."

"Are you proud of us for telling them off and catching most of them?" Petey said.

I was silent probably for too long.

"Lorraine?" Petey said.

"Did you tell the guy Ricky was at my place?"

"Oh, shit, Lorraine," Petey said. "Everybody and their brother knows you got that boy at your place. Do you think he's headed there?"

"I don't know, but I'm going to find out."

Ricky? What about Momma and Allan? Will the bastard kill them?

I tried calling Momma from my cell phone.

No answer.

She probably turned the damn thing off trying to save the battery.

I called the landline.

No answer.

Chapter Twenty-Three

I HIT REDIAL again and again. Still no answer.

I floored the accelerator, fishtailed in the gravel on the side of the road, sped home and all the way up my driveway. I pulled up and parked next to a dark green truck that looked a lot like Lewis's. I didn't see him or Petey around. *Wow, he got here fast.*

There was no sign of Dad or Kenny or either of their trucks. Momma's station wagon was gone too, but I could see where she had last parked. Our charcoal grill lay in the grass like a wounded beetle.

Weird. The dogs didn't come running. I heard them bark from behind the barn doors. *We never keep them locked up. Momma and Dad wouldn't do that. Something fishy's going on.* My mouth went dry, because my breathing came fast.

When I got to the front porch the screen door was ajar, and the inside door gaped. No lights on in the kitchen or dining room, but the living room ceiling light was on. It was getting close to dark. In a half hour or so, I knew the yard lights would splash on once they were activated by the timer Dad set to coincide with what the *Farmers' Almanac* said about sunset and sunrise.

"Ricky?" I knew Ricky couldn't answer me, but I felt like I needed to call to him. *How did Lewis get here so fast? I thought he was chasing after the other guy who helped beat Ricky.* The porch boards creaked and the screen door squeaked as I entered the kitchen. The house felt lonely, hollow. *What am I gonna see?* I felt along the wall for the light switch, still scanning the rest of the house as best I could. I flipped on the light in the kitchen. The coiled fluorescent bulb buzzed a bit and hesitated before it burned out. I tripped over a kitchen chair that had already been overturned. *Momma never leaves a mess in the kitchen and Dad wouldn't risk it either.* I walked through the dining room trying to get a glimpse at the living room. "Ricky? Are you home? Where's Momma?" I stood in the living room doorway trying to act casual.

"Ricky? Ricky?" He was there, but he wasn't alone.

The room was a mess. Ricky's cosmetology case was like an open mouth and his favorite brushes and doodads were scattered across the floor like missing teeth. The end table had been overturned. The coffee table had been pulled away from the couch where we'd made up a bed for Ricky. The blankets, pillows, and Grandma's quilt were in a heap on the floor. A pitcher of ice water had been spilled. The water soaked into the hardwood floor. A few ice cubes remained, but had melted to pebbles. Someone had bashed the boom box. Shattered CDs littered the floor like glass.

"Come in, Lorraine. You're early. I'd planned to be finished before you got home." *Finished what?* Lewis sat next to Ricky on the couch holding him upright. Ricky's mouth was bleeding. Then I was shoved further into the room. I snuck a quick look back and Petey blocked the doorway.

"Did you get those college boys? Did you call the sheriff?"

Lewis laughed. "I reckon those boys are back at college enjoying date rape and slapping one another's ass on the football field like a bunch of faggots." He took a pull from the bottle of beer he had beside him.

I'd been running on fumes for days. I couldn't organize my thoughts or senses. I couldn't make sense of what I was seeing.

Lewis stood up. He pointed to the spot where he'd been sitting. "Come on, have a seat by your little faggot friend."

"I'm okay standing."

Lewis stiffened and turn red. "This is my operation, Lorraine. I'm the foreman. If I tell you to sit on the couch, you God damn better sit on the couch!"

"Okay, okay. I'm sorry." I sat down and turned to Ricky. "Are you all right?"

"Of course, he's all right. Petey and I were just having a talk with Ricky. We need an advanced showing of what Ricky will say tomorrow. Was it an act of God, an angel of the Lord?"

"You think it God or an angel of the Lord beat Ricky? How much have you been drinking, Lewis?"

"Lorraine, you aren't an expert on everything. There are men, godly men who know about the acts of God. What happened to Ricky could be an act of God and Ricky needs to bear witness."

"How can you possibly call the beating he got an act of God? God is love, Lewis."

Lewis ignored my logic. "Actually, it's good you're here, Lorraine. You can use your superior knowledge of animals and perform a little procedure on Ricky." He reached out to hand me an instrument.

Oh Christ. He had a wire cutter like you'd use on a car.

"I'm not using that dirty thing on Ricky. It's not intended for the delicate wires used for orthodontic brackets." I thought I was being reasonable explaining the obvious.

Lewis rubbed his face, took another drink of his beer, and threw the bottle against the wall just above mine and Ricky's head. We both startled as we were splattered with glass and beer foam.

"You just don't get it, Lorraine. You aren't the boss here. I don't give a shit about all the things you think you know. You cut the wires because I told you to."

"I'm not doing that." I turned to Ricky and whispered, "You be ready. When I say run, you scoot across the room to the armchair."

"What are you saying?" Lewis was on me then. He pulled me up by my shirt. The tips of the wire cutters went through the fabric and cut my chest as Lewis tossed me across the room to where Petey stood. "If you won't do it, I will." He knelt on the couch by Ricky. He grabbed Ricky by the chin and turned his head. He pushed Ricky's lips apart.

When I tried to step forward, Petey grabbed my arm. "Stay right where you are."

Plink! Lewis clipped a wire. Ricky whimpered. Tears streamed down his face. His eyes rolled back, and I thought he would pass out from the pain and fear but Lewis propped him up again like a hand puppet. "Lorraine, give your cell phone to Petey or I will break Ricky's neck right now."

I handed my phone to Petey. Lewis nodded at him and Petey dropped my phone to the floor and stepped on it.

Shit. It took an act of congress to get my first phone. I kept my eyes on Lewis and Ricky.

"Don't bother running to the landline in the kitchen. That contraption is having some wiring problems too. Wakey, wakey, fairy boy." Lewis shook Ricky at the shoulders. "We're almost done."

"Stop this. Lewis, Petey! When Momma gets here she is going to rip you a new one!"

"Your fat assed momma's not coming home for a long while. There's an emergency at the clinic. Didn't you know?" Lewis kissed Ricky's cheek and smiled at me.

"Momma wouldn't leave Ricky alone. She'd have waited until I was home."

"She'd leave wee Ricky alone if she got a call about an emergency at the clinic and her daughter texted her she'd be right home to sit with Ricky."

"I never texted that to Momma."

Lewis pursed his lips and nodded. "Well the text came from your phone."

How in the hell? Then I remembered. He'd taken my phone at the Lake Tavern to put his number in. Damn, he'd been busy.

Lewis kept talking. "What with that emergency and the fire at the lumber yard, your folks will be tied up a long while."

"Fire? Was anyone hurt?"

"I don't know, but my guess it wasn't too good for your dad. He coughs almost every time he talks. He's a smoker like me. Filthy habit. That's why I chew more often now." Lewis put a plug of tobacco in his cheek.

Tears dripped down my face onto my shirt. I didn't know what to do next. I wanted to call Momma and Dad. I wanted to help Ricky. "Just leave. Go as far away as your truck will take you. You don't have to take this any further."

Lewis quickly clipped another wire and then lowered the clipper as he gestured toward me. "That's where you're wrong again, Lorraine the lesbian. We should not have to leave this county or this country. Godly men like me and Petey here are instruments of God in taking this country back. We're helping to purify America."

"What are you talking about, Lewis?" I stepped closer, but Petey kept hold of my arm. Then I had the sudden instinct to change directions and buy some time, so I could think. "What happened to the dogs?"

"Christ, even your dogs are naïve and stupid." Lewis laughed. He drank again. "A friendly voice and a few wieners and the dogs went right into the barn. I hope they have some water and it isn't too hot for them. I hate to see poor, dumb animals suffer."

"Speaking of dumb animals, how can you call yourselves Godly men? Petey raped a minor. This is your chance to get away, boys. I already called the sheriff."

Petey twitched, visibly shaken. He seemed to vacillate between a desire to hold on to me or go to Lewis.

"Don't try to bluff us, Lorraine." Lewis took his arm from around Ricky, sat forward, but kept a hand tight on Ricky's wrist.

"It's true, Petey. I called the sheriff and told him about you being Addie's boyfriend right after you let me know. Shit, sex with a minor." I shook my head back and forth.

"I didn't do anything to Addie she wasn't willing to do, Lorraine." Petey put his hands on the sides of his head and swayed back and forth from one leg to the other. "She's sixteen. Sixteen is legal in Minnesota." Petey panicked. He moved closer to Lewis, pushing me to the side as he went. I stumbled and fell against the armchair.

"Doesn't matter. She's in care. She's considered vulnerable. She can't give her consent to adults to be sexual with her." I riled Petey a little more. "Best if you just make a run for it. Don't add murder to the mess you're already in."

Petey stood over Lewis. "I didn't sign on for this, Lewis. He said if we helped with this, we'd be done. Neither of us would be in any trouble. Now I'm hearing I'm about to be arrested, Lewis."

"Shut up, Petey! Don't you get that she's just winding you up? We finish this, Petey, and we're done. We can go back to like it was before." He let go of Ricky. Ricky slid farther away from Lewis. "Petey, we just need to find out what he remembers. We weren't there. He ain't going to finger us. We do our jobs and we'll have money, get our own land and spread."

"Lewis, tell me again about the ranch." Petey swayed back and forth from one foot to the other.

"We're going to buy a piece of land." Lewis droned on like he recited a familiar bedtime story. "We'll park the trailer on the land until we can build something bigger. We'll have cattle—no milking—beef cattle. Maybe hogs and chickens too. Hell, rabbits, chimpanzees, and ostriches if you want, Petey."

This was my chance. I reached behind the armchair and pulled the shotgun from its hiding place. I pumped a shell into the chamber and fired it into the ceiling, chambered another load, and moved forward. "Ricky, run!" Ricky scampered from the couch to the armchair behind me. "Petey, get your ass on the floor. Lewis, keep your hands where I can see them." I pointed the gun at them. I'd never pointed a gun at a person in my life and hoped I never would again. Petey stood in a soporific daze, slack jawed and confused.

Lewis reluctantly, slowly raised his hands. He smiled. "Lorraine, Lorraine, Lorraine. You got your daddy's Winchester. A fine piece of weaponry." He began to lower his hands as he talked.

"Keep your hands up!" *Don't make me shoot.* It would have been a fine time for me to demand Lewis's cell phone to call the sheriff, or Momma or Dad or Twitch or anybody who might help, but I didn't like the way Lewis smiled. And definitely didn't want to get very close to him. Besides, my hands were full and Ricky couldn't talk or work a cell phone with his broken fingers.

"Double barrel, pump action shotgun. It has its advantages and disadvantages, of course." Lewis raised his hands again.

"I know what you're getting at, Lewis. It can only hold three shells. That might be considered a disadvantage. I already fired one in the ceiling and chambered another round. I either have one or two shots left. You can risk it I suppose, but the great advantage of this gun is at this close range it's going to do a lot of damage. One shell or two, the next one I fire is going into you." I raised the gun higher to site him in.

"Lewis, let's get out of here!" Petey pleaded.

Lewis ignored Petey. His smile was gone. "I don't believe you have the guts to shoot anyone. I know you don't have the balls for it."

"Dislodging the stuck calf you messed up was hard, cutting Killer's horn off was scary, dealing with McGerber took courage. Believe me, I've got all the balls I need to shoot you bullies." I stood, feet apart, like I had seen Dad do when he shot a rifle. I tried to keep from shaking or passing out.

Petey scampered on his hands and knees out of the room. I watched him from the corner of my eye and heard the screen door slam and he called for Lewis to come with him.

Apparently, some of Lewis's bravado drained away once his minion ran away. He rose from the couch with his hands still in the air and bowed and shook his head. "This has all been an unfortunate misunderstanding." Lewis smiled, but he was obviously nervous. "My job was just to help Ricky bear witness to what might have been an act of God as I hear it." He slowly edged toward the door. I kept the gun trained on him. On his way out of the living room he flipped off the light.

I left the light off. I watched him through the window. He got in his truck with Petey. The dome light in his truck came on. He jabbered into his cell phone as he sped away from the house.

Damn. I should have taken his phone.

"Ricky, are you all right? We've got to get out of here!" I leaned the shotgun against the couch. Ricky couldn't talk even though some of the wires were cut. He cried, shook his head no, and pulled at me. "Okay, okay, sit down. Calm yourself a while, but then we've got to get out of here." I didn't bother to turn on the lights again. Somehow, it felt like the darkness protected us from the rest of the world for at least a minute.

"We've got to tell the sheriff about Lewis and Petey." I helped Ricky back to his nest on the couch and sat between him and the shotgun. I was jumpy as a meth addict needing a fix. I didn't want to stick around here.

Sounds from out in the yard added to my near hysteria. The dogs barked again from inside the barn. A car door slammed. Footsteps on the porch. *Great. I hope that's Momma.* I had no energy to get up and see for myself.

"Ricky? Are you home?" someone called. The voice was false, the tone all wrong—sing-songy high and mocking, like he called a dog. The voice sorta familiar, but creepy. The hairs stood up on my neck. I didn't speak or move.

The screen door slammed. He was inside my house. "Ricky? It's time to come to Jesus. Too bad you're all alone. I saw that bossy nurse and that little brat in town." He walked through the kitchen. "Never send boys to do a man's job. That's what I always say."

Boys? Boys? What's he talking about? Lewis and Petey. He's here to finish. I couldn't breathe.

"Maybe I could send your little faggot ass to heaven before I dispatch your wicked soul to hell." He laughed. He moved to the dining room.

I couldn't identify who he was, just male, tall, but I knew his voice and he'd come for Ricky.

He moved over in front of the picture window but facing the couch. Just then the yard lights turned on as scheduled and the man was back lit. I couldn't see his face, only his outline. He wore a suit and he carried an axe.

Shit. Shit. Shit. I put my hand over my mouth to keep from screaming.

"Ricky, I'm back to see you again. Do you want to tell me how pretty my eyes are? Will you stroke the gray at my temples and say how distinguished I look? I do wish you could talk and coo a bit before I silence you forever." He moved closer to the end of the couch and passed the axe from one hand to the other. "Oh well, such is life. It's time to have the rest of your coming to Jesus. Pardon the pun." He felt along the wall, probably searching for the light switch. "Let me see your little faggot face."

I don't remember grabbing the shotgun. It was already there in my hands. I fired at the arm and hand holding the ax. The ax fell to the floor.

I COULDN'T GET away from him, the smell of gunpowder, and the darkness of the room fast enough. I pulled Ricky along with me as I ran out of the house like we were being chased by the devil himself. I shoved Ricky into my truck from the driver's side. My keys were still in the ignition of my truck. I ground the starter, turning over the engine and turning the key again. I left the driver's side door open, the dome light was on, and I thought there was someone else in the car with me. I looked behind me.

No one's there.

I glanced in the mirror again. My face was speckled with blood. I hurried to close the door as I backed up my truck without properly checking my mirrors and slammed into the truck the axman must have driven. I scrutinized the vehicle more closely as I pulled forward and looped around. It looked like the fancy black truck I saw at McGerber's place.

Oh Christ, I killed J.C. McGerber.

I needed to find Momma, and Allan. I needed my dad and Twitch. I put my truck in drive and headed toward Bend.

I HAD NO memory of the drive, but I'd made it a thousand times before. I pulled my truck to the curb in front of the café. I rolled down the window and shouted to the first person I saw to use their phone.

Just then, Dad's truck peeled out of the clinic parking lot. Momma was driving. She drove the truck down the sidewalk by the bank, past Art's Barber Shop, did a U-turn, and looped back. Dad and Allan pinballed in the passenger seat as Momma drove across Bob and Fran's grocery store parking lot, over Welinski's lawn, over the park horseshoe pits and onto Berkey Street.

What's she doing? "Never mind, here's your phone." I sped away after Momma. I honked my horn until she screeched to a stop in front of Pastor Grind's church. Grind's car. *That's never good news.* Grind's car was parked in front of the church alongside Twitch's Jeep.

I parked and bolted out of my truck. "Dad, Momma, Christ, you won't..."

"Lorraine, watch your language." Momma pulled out her notebook and mumbled something about the terrible day she'd had, a false emergency at the clinic, fire at the lumber yard, and then she stopped. "Whose blood is that? You're going to need to soak that shirt."

I slapped Momma's notebook to the ground. "Don't worry about my shirt, Momma. Help me get Ricky someplace safe!"

"The church is safe. It's why I called you to bring him here. You'd know that if you answered your phone." Momma peered into my truck cab and put her arms out to Ricky.

Dad picked up Momma's notebook and handed it to her. "Peggy, let me do that." He put Allan in my arms, eased by Momma, and reached into the truck to gently help Ricky slide across the seat.

"You crying?" Allan touched my face.

"Yep. Everybody poops and everybody cries." Any mention of poop made the little bugger laugh. I needed somebody to have a reason to laugh.

Momma got a better look at Ricky. "That's Ricky's blood on your shirt, Lorraine. What happened?" She licked her thumb and wiped at my face. "Get in the church. Pastor Grind has to talk with all of us." Momma started up the steps; one hand had a tight grip on the railing and the other hand had a tight grip on me. I carried Allan and Dad carried Ricky.

"No way in hell I'm going in there." It shouldn't surprise me, but neither my momma nor dad listened to a word I said. Momma pulled me along as she went right up those church steps and pounded on the door of the church, yelling for Grind to let us in.

Only Allan paid any attention. "No way in hell."

Momma let go of my arm and took Allan from me.

Grind opened the door and waved Momma, Dad, Allan, and Ricky into the church. He cast his eyes directly at me.

"Well, Lorraine? There isn't much time."

I walked up a few steps and went back down to the sidewalk. *It's a trap sure as hell. His accomplices have failed. Now he's going to kill us.* I heard squealing tires from Main Street. *How many people are doing McGerber's bidding?* I thought about the shotgun in the truck, but it only had one bullet left and I'd forgotten more shells. I hustled into the church. At best all I could do was plead for them to save Allan and bring him up in the church. He hadn't hurt anybody. Maybe Jolene or Charity could raise him, or Marin could find him a good home.

Grind waited for me. He locked the doors behind me and hustled me into the sanctuary. The ceiling lights were on, but there were candles lit near the front too. *Oh crap, it's like TV where nobody kills anybody quick. Everything's a big production with speeches and backstory. I'm waiting for organ music.*

Twitch talked quietly to Ricky by the communion table. He helped Ricky climb up on the table and lay down. Twitch stood over him and then he put on a blue surgical gown and white gloves. Another man in a suit stood by Twitch with his back to me. I ran down the aisle.

"What are you doing? Don't kill Ricky!"

"Lorraine?" Twitch turned to me.

The man holding Ricky's upper body turned. *J.C. McGerber. Son of a bitch. If I didn't shoot McGerber, who'd I shoot?*

Dad held a candle closer. Momma had Allan pressed against her.

Twitch used his gloved fingers to push back Ricky's lips. He held small shears in his other hand. "Christ, what a mess. Some of these wires look like they've been chewed off. They're poking right into his cheek."

I yelled again, "Don't kill Ricky!"

"We're not going to kill Ricky." Twitch took his hands away from Ricky's mouth. "The doctor said Ricky's wires could come out tomorrow. I got some tools from an oral surgeon I know. We're doing it a day early." He shook out his shoulder, dabbed on Ricky's lips with a sterile bandage he soaked with water. "I cleared it with Doctor Jonas at the hospital." Twitch winked at me. "Let's see what this boy knows about who hurt him."

"It was Lewis and Petey." I stepped closer to Ricky.

Twitch stopped his assault on Ricky's mouth again. "How do you know?"

"They were waiting for me at the farm. It was Lewis who made a mess of Ricky's mouth already. I think they planned to kill us both." I looked at Dad. "I scared them off with the shotgun you hid in the living room."

Momma swatted Dad. "You hid a shotgun in my living room?" She reached toward her purse.

Dad pointed at Momma. "Don't you even think about writing that in your notebook. There's no time for that nonsense."

"Today, ladies!" Twitch yelled. "You can sort out your decorating scheme and sin tallies later. For right now we've got this to deal with." He applied a topical anesthetic gel onto Ricky's gums and inner cheeks. "This will numb your mouth. We'll get the sheriff to scoop up those knuckleheads, but we aren't waiting any longer for someone to try to hurt him again...or hurt anybody else." Twitch swallowed hard, glanced at me and back at Ricky. "Ricky can tell us everything that happened and get this mess sorted."

Plink. Twitch snipped one wire and then another. Ricky moaned and groaned.

"Almost finished, son." Twitch touched Ricky's shoulder.

Ricky's eyes were wide and teary. They rolled back in his head.

I held Ricky's hand. "It had to be Lewis and Petey. Why else would they have come after Ricky at the farm?" Ricky squeezed my hand as much as he could with broken fingers.

Plink, plink, his jaws were loose from each other, but disinclined to open after being closed so long I suppose.

"I don't think anybody's saying you're wrong about Lewis and Petey, Lorraine." Dad offered Ricky water from a cup. Most of it spilled down his neck and front. "We just need to hear the whole story and get an official statement to the sheriff."

McGerber hovered. He carefully wiped Ricky's mouth with a pressed white cloth handkerchief he took from his suit pocket. "It's okay, son. Take your time. We have plenty of water for you, whatever you need."

What's McGerber playing at? I don't trust him. At any moment, he was going to grab Ricky's head and break his neck.

Twitch told Ricky not to try to speak yet. He needed to put some dental rubber bands on Ricky's arch bars—the apparatus that kept Ricky's jaw in place since the break. "Don't worry, Ricky. I watched a YouTube video on how to do this." Twitch grinned.

I might faint. Despite the local anesthetic tears still streamed from Ricky's eyes and his nose ran.

Once the elastic bands were on, Ricky could open his mouth a little and try speaking. He could if he was willing to. I had my doubts even though he'd promised me he would.

We waited for him to speak, surrounding him as he was stretched out on the communion table. Momma passed Allan over to Dad. She got out her notebook. She gave Dad a look. Then she licked the lead of the pencil she had tied to the notebook with string. She readied for dictation. She would take the names and she would bring retribution.

Ricky's breathing was quick, his eyes watered and darted from McGerber to Twitch to Pastor Grind, to Momma, to Dad, to Allan, and to me and around the circle again like a spinning bottle. The last time through his gaze stopped at me.

"Lorraine, I think he wants to tell you." Dad nodded at me.

Great. I leaned over closer to Ricky. His lips were dry and cracked. Blood caked the corner of his mouth again and the inside of his mouth appeared inflamed. I leaned even closer. He whispered, but I didn't catch it. Closer. His chapped lips were against my outer ear—shivers raced down my arms as his breath fluttered against my ear and my neck. He whispered. His sentences were short. His breath was humid against my ear. He told me what had happened. He whispered the truth and a name I didn't imagine.

Even more confused and scared, I ran the story over in my mind: the shiny black truck, the familiar voice, the suit. I did what made sense to me. I squeezed Ricky's arm. I asked Twitch to stay with Ricky and McGerber. I asked Momma, Dad, and Pastor Grind to come out to the foyer with me. Their patience with me grew thin.

"For God's sake, Lorraine," Momma said. "What did he say?"

Oh, crap. It's not going to get easier by waiting longer. "He said some college boys followed him and pulled him out of the car, but he doesn't remember anything after that until he woke up in the hospital."

"Christ, I never expected that." Dad wiped his forehead with his handkerchief.

"He may not remember, but I think it's pretty clear there were other people involved." I searched their sad, disbelieving faces. "Where's McGerber's brother?"

Grind spoke first. "Why do you ask about McGerber's brother, Lorraine?"

"Because I think he's behind this beating and the attempt to make Ricky talk out at the farm. Lewis made it sound like he and Petey were getting paid to see what Ricky remembered."

"You think that was Warren McGerber?" Dad put a hand on my shoulder.

Grind sat down on the wooden bench in the foyer like his legs couldn't hold him any longer.

"Well, I'm going to give both McGerbers a piece of my mind." Momma moved toward the sanctuary again, but Grind called her back.

"I'll deal with J.C. We've got to notify the sheriff right away," Grind said. "He could be anywhere. He could come to this church this very minute to finish the job."

"Actually, Warren McGerber can't finish the job." I pulled at my messy curls. *I'm going to vomit.*

"How do you know he isn't coming here, Lorraine?" Momma looked at me with her brow furrowed.

"Because he's on our living room floor."

"What's Warren McGerber doing in our living room?"

"The gun."

"You shot someone, Lorraine?" Dad put his hand over his mouth.

Momma appeared speechless for once.

"I think I killed him. He came to the farm after Lewis and Petey left. He had an ax. He talked about dispatching Ricky's soul to hell." My eyes darted from Momma to Dad and to Grind and around the horn again. None of them could help me. *The truth will set you free.* "I shot him. I shot him because I thought Ricky and I were both in danger for our lives. I shot him and got Ricky out of there."

For a moment we all stood statue still. Momma went to motion first. She ran to Pastor Grind's office. "I'll call for an ambulance and the sheriff."

"I'll turn myself in." I cried like I'd never be able to stop. "I'm sorry."

Pastor Grind stood up, straightened his suit, and approached me. "Oh, Lorraine, I'm so sorry. How frightening. Are you okay?"

I nodded. We both stared over to where J.C. McGerber stood with Twitch and Ricky.

I took Pastor Grind's arm. "It was Petey, McGerber's farmhand, who had sex with Addie. He's her boyfriend. He didn't know she was pregnant. Do you want me to talk to McGerber? Tell him about his brother? I need to apologize...for accusing him of hurting Addie." *Please, please, please, don't make me do it.*

Grind firmly grasped my shoulder. "You're not going to tell him. I'll tell him. Lorraine. I don't know how exactly, but I'll do it. Violence begat violence. It's an old, familiar story. You know, Lorraine, J.C. and I set out this evening to get Ricky and you to safety from whomever would come back to hurt him again. We wanted to make this church a true sanctuary."

I didn't know that, and I didn't understand it.

"This is going to be a shock for J.C., but it doesn't change what we intended to do. It's going to be okay. We're all going to be okay."

Pastor Grind returned to where Twitch stood vigil over Ricky. I watched as Grind said something to McGerber. McGerber had been on his flip phone. He pocketed it and followed Grind away from the others. They stood together, a stained-glass window depicting Christ's broken body as a backdrop, and Pastor Grind talked. I didn't hear what Grind said to McGerber, but from where I stood I saw the way the weight of the truth and what must come next pulled all McGerber's facial features down. His spine seemed like it was being yanked to earth by a magnet from the core of the world. His disappointment and loss shone on his face. I knew his heart seized and his brain forgot its function. I knew because I had lost Becky and there were no words to make it easy or hurt less.

Chapter Twenty-Four

I WAITED UNTIL Pastor Grind had moved away from J.C. McGerber. I went to him slowly hoping he'd clue me in if he was going to throttle me before I got too close.

"I'm sorry I blamed you for hurting Addie." I never imagined myself apologizing to McGerber for anything. "Petey's Addie's boyfriend. It was wrong for him to have sex with Addie, and it was also wrong that it was allowed to happen right under your nose."

He glanced at me and looked away again without speaking, nodding. He slowly digested my words.

"Mister McGerber, it was wrong of me to assume you hurt Addie. I hope you can find it in your heart to...forgive me."

He looked at me then. He gazed at me saying the sort of thing he expected of people including himself.

"You were wrong, Miss Tyler, but I can see how you could've made the mistake."

"Mister McGerber, I'm sorry you lost your brother. I'm sorry for my part in it."

"It's so strange. I just called my brother before Allister told me what had happened. Warren didn't pick up, of course. I left him a message that the boy couldn't remember his attackers. I was certain he'd want to know. He's interested in this community."

Yeah, he was interested all right. It's all self-interest. "I can't say I have any love for him given all he did, but I'm sorry for your loss. I know what that's like."

"I know you do, child. Thank you." He looked away as he wiped his eyes. "I think you and I both wanted to help our family find a better path. We are joined together in our mutual failure."

"I'm just curious. Why'd you help Ricky? I thought you were against queers like us."

"That pastor there. He convicted my heart and told me what he understood to be God's way. He said, 'we should never lose a chance to show mercy so that we too will be shown mercy.' Lord, have mercy on us all."

I wasn't ready to pronounce anything a success or failure. Thankfully, Ricky was alive and safe. Next, I went to say my piece to Pastor Grind, but before I got to him somebody pounded on the church door, yelling to get in.

Dad unlocked the door and peered out. There's no peephole in church doors. The yeller pushed the door open.

Who in the heck is...wait a minute?

The man strode in adjusting his suit at the lapels as he brushed his silver hair back with his hand.

J.C. McGerber stepped up to him. "Warren?"

"My brother in the Lord. Good to see you, J.C." The man dwarfed J.C. McGerber a bit, but even a casual observer could see the resemblance.

Warren McGerber? I recognized his voice. *He* had been the man I heard talking to Grind that day. I obviously hadn't shot him. Who had I shot?

"Warren, you're alive." McGerber touched his brother's arm.

"Of course, I'm alive." He slapped J.C. McGerber on the shoulder. "There's too much work to be done for the Godly to tarry."

"Warren, did you beat this boy?" Grind stumbled forward, obviously shaken having seen someone raised from the dead.

"Did he say I beat him?" Warren looked from Grind to Ricky.

Ricky shook his head no.

"Ricky states he doesn't remember, but Lorraine said you came after Ricky at their farm and she had to shoot you." Pastor Grind lost all color in his face like he'd seen a ghost.

"Do I look like I have been shot? I tell you, gentlemen and ladies, I have come to restore Bend and communities like it to good, family values. I have no reason to soil my hands with violence or sloth." Warren moved among us like we were part of a rally he'd organized to support his campaign. He was schilling for votes and searching for a baby to kiss.

"Who beat Ricky after those college boys pulled him from the car?" Dad stayed on point.

"Perhaps it was an act of God." Warren peered into heaven I guess.

"That's what Lewis said." I whispered to Dad.

J.C. McGerber turned to me. "Lorraine, how could you make me think Warren was dead and that he had committed such an act?"

"I thought..."

I didn't get to finish. Momma came over to me. "Why'd you tell us a tale about shooting that man, Lorraine?"

"It's not a tale. It's the truth. Look at the blood on my shirt. I thought it had to be Warren McGerber." I looked into her eyes. "There was someone else involved in this and they either orchestrated it or did the beating or both.

Ricky doesn't remember because there was ketamine in his system."

"What did you say, Lorraine?" Momma's brow furrowed enough to hold loose change.

"Whoever did this had access to ketamine. It wasn't me and it wasn't Twitch. The man knew that drug would impede Ricky's memory."

"Ketamine? Oh no, Lorraine." Momma covered her mouth with her hand. "I'll call dispatch to see if the sheriff and ambulance have made it to the farm."

"Momma, do you know who I shot?"

"I think I do." She hugged me. "I'm glad you're safe. It's going to be okay. I've got to call the sheriff myself."

I went over to Ricky. I hugged him. "I'm sorry I've been pushing you to tell us who hurt you. I understand better now why it was hard."

"What about Warren? Do you still believe he is involved? He flirted with me, Lorraine." Ricky and I watched the McGerber men and Pastor Grind talk about signs and flyers McGerber wanted distributed.

"I don't have any proof unless Lewis and Petey or the guy at the farm know something and will testify. If Lewis and Petey are smart they're nowhere near here. I don't know if the guy at the farm is in any shape to talk even if he were willing."

Ricky stared into my eyes. Tears dripped down his face. He swallowed hard. Through a tender, aching mouth he said, "Lorraine, you look awful. Don't you at least try to brush your hair? Your skin's so dry."

"I told you I can't wait for you to give me a facial and work on my hair." Ricky was healing.

Warren and J.C. McGerber were leaving. "Come on, brother. I need your help. My signs came in. I have them in the truck." J.C. scowled at me but didn't say anything. Warren smiled in my direction. The feeling of vomit came back.

Grind came over to where Ricky and I talked.

I didn't know what he had to say to me after Warren McGerber's grand entrance and speech. Still, he had tried to help Ricky by giving him sanctuary in the church while Twitch cut the wires. The cost of it for him was not lost on me.

"Thanks for opening the church, Pastor Grind."

"Thank you, Pastor," Ricky said.

I couldn't help myself. Grind had been such a pain in the ass to me. After all his condemnations of queers I still couldn't get my head around him having saved Ricky. "Why'd you do it, Pastor Grind? After all you said..."

"I went to see Ricky earlier in the day, see him for myself." Grind had tears in his eyes. "I don't know what I expected. Horns, maybe? Certainly not what I found. He was so small and broken and bruised. All I could think of..." He broke off. I heard the choking in his throat as he spoke. "All I could think about was my Charity—that someone could think it was God's will to beat her, hurt her. I'm ashamed. Isn't it something that I never thought what it would look like to strike out literally against sin?"

I got teary again.

"There's a New Testament story in Acts chapter ten. Peter, a devout Jew, is invited to the home of a Gentile."

"Yeah, Cornelius, the soldier." I sat down because it sounded like Grind was going to be windy.

"You know the story, Lorraine?"

"Of course, I know it. I've been at Sunday school since I was little. You know, Pastor Grind, I believe in God. I just don't believe God would make me as I am, queer, and condemn me for the same thing."

Grind smiled. "Have you meditated on the story of Peter and Cornelius?"

"I don't know that I've meditated on it, but I know the story. Peter was hungry. He had a vision of this big sheet with all these animals that weren't on the Jewish menu for approved foods. A voice said, 'Kill and eat.' Peter objected because the animals were unclean. The voice said, 'Don't call anything impure that God has made clean.' This happens like three times. Then Peter gets invited to the home of Cornelius, a Gentile. Jews weren't supposed to go to the homes of Gentiles, but Peter goes. Peter understood the visions as a message from God that God decides what is clean and unclean, what is pure and impure, and God doesn't show favoritism. God accepts people from all nations who fear God and do what is right."

Grind smiled. "For that time period, there were four-footed animals, reptiles, and birds on the sheet that God reclassified from unclean to clean to show Peter the spirit of the Gospel. I wonder what would be on the sheet in our modern times?"

"You think there'd be queers, Pastor? Hopefully, the voice doesn't say, 'Kill and eat.'"

"I believe, I have always believed it my duty to drive evil out of the church, out of this world, and I had learned that homosexuality was a type of evil. But when I beheld the boy, Ricky, I thought of Charity or you for that matter, and I can't call you evil. I don't understand why God made you like you are, but I don't doubt you were made by God." Grind's voice squeaked. "My heart was convicted; and I came to understand that hate and violence are clearly the worst evil. This church"—he surveyed the stained-glass windows, the banners, the cross above the altar—"this church will be used for sanctuary for as long as I'm here to offer it. God will judge what and whomever are pure or impure."

"That's a good thing," I said. I was crying and so was Ricky. "What about what I said about Warren McGerber? Do you believe me?"

"I think Warren McGerber requires closer scrutiny. I will fight against him if he is peddling fear and hatred in the name of God. I will not let that stand. Which is the long way of saying I believe you, Lorraine."

I suppose it was the shock of him helping Ricky and believing me, but I kept talking. "I think Charity and I broke up."

"Am I understanding you correctly?"

"Yes sir. I suppose you're relieved about that?"

"Maybe. I'm not so positive about what I am any more when it comes to the details of all these things." He put his hand on my shoulder gently and leaned in a bit. "I do know long-distance relationships are difficult." He took his hand away. "Charity says she's going to Europe. Also, you should know that Jolene will be home this weekend and she's bringing a boyfriend along."

"Wow, have you met him?"

"This will be the first time." Grind raised his eyebrows and sighed. "If you aren't too busy I know she'd like to see her old friend and I'd like to hear what you think of this boyfriend. I admit I'm not too objective."

"I'm probably not too objective either."

"I'm counting on it, Lorraine." Then Pastor Grind smiled warmly at me and touched Ricky's shoulder before he walked to the front of the church and began tidying the communion table.

Chapter Twenty-Five

MOMMA CAME TO stand by Ricky and me. She blew raspberries on Allan's cheek and neck as she held him. She shifted him to her hip and gave me a quick, one-armed hug. She didn't say anything at first. Then she hugged me again and said, "I'm glad you're safe." Like she caught herself being too mushy she added, "There's lots of work to be done." She moved Allan to her other hip and took Ricky's arm. "We're meeting Kenny and Ramona at Big Will's Diner. Big Will agreed to give us the place for a private party to celebrate your return to more solid foods."

Of course, Momma's first thought after safety was to feed us.

"I'm sure it will be adequate, but never as good as your cooking," Ricky mumbled.

Momma squeezed the little suck-up again. She turned back to me. "Big Will said he'd be ready for us in about an hour. Your dad and Twitch headed out to our place to meet the sheriff."

What she didn't need to say was she wanted me cleaned up and to make certain there wasn't evidence of what I did all over our living room when she brought Allan and Ricky home again. She'd already figured out who I'd shot, so had I, but neither of us said it out loud. "I still had to give a statement to the sheriff, but hopefully once he sees the ax I won't be in trouble."

"Here." Momma handed me her notebook. "There's Ricky's statement written down word for word."

"But are you sure you want me to have your notebook?"

"I don't need it anymore."

Chapter Twenty-Six

I DROVE AWAY from Grind's church through the town of Bend, Minnesota, population three fifty, when everyone was home for Christmas. There were a few cars at the three Bend hardware stores and a few parked at the Ponderosa Café, but the only busy parking lot was at the Municipal Liquor Store. Every block or two my headlights reflected off newly planted yard signs. "Warren McGerber for State Senate 20—: Boots on the ground to protect America!"

My battered, blue truck kicked up gravel and dust as I wound between paved and country gravel roads. Even in the inky night I could picture the patchwork quilt fields, stands of pines and mixed groves of oaks, maples, birch, and elm trees, and generously placed clean lakes, meandering rivers, and serpentine creeks. I thought about the people of Bend. They're nice, hard-working people who generally get along with one another on the safe topics: weather, farming being hard, working hard being virtuous, hunting being necessary, and loyalty to all Bend High School Pioneer sports teams. The topics of religion, politics, abortion, and bedrooms generally sparked a polarization that mimicked much of the United States.

If I was right, Warren McGerber was mounting a campaign couched in hate and fear. He wanted to take over the hearts of people in Bend and towns like it. I couldn't prove he orchestrated the attack on Ricky, but

Grind believed me and said he'd fight. I refused to let myself believe the people of Bend could be totally fooled by hate speech.

I was queer and since being outed by my momma a few years back, my place in Bend was strained. I detected some fear that could be dressed up as hate. I survived the uncertainty and took refuge in the air of indifference and polite tolerance and hoped to be embraced someday. Still, the majority of the folks were doing the best they could with what they believed and thought they knew for certain. *For certain none of us are perfect.*

I had one more responsibility to Ricky. I went to see Russ. I found the big man in his garage working on a car under the shop light. He wiped his hands on a rag as he walked away from the car he was disemboweling. He came over to me.

"How's Ricky?"

"He can talk now."

"Oh?" Russ stared at the ground. "He have a lot to say?" He spit a wad of gum into the dirt.

"Yeah, you know he said some interesting things. I think the most interesting thing he said was that he loved you." *It's strange to declare another's love, but I saw how it was necessary.*

Russ's back was to me. He trembled through his navy work shirt. Then the big old grease monkey dissolved in tears. "I let him down. I was a coward."

"Yeah, that's true and Ricky loves you."

He cried a while and I let him. After a few minutes, he talked.

"You know we'd all been going to the Lake Tavern since Kenny invited us? Kenny, Ricky, and me. It was fun, you know? We drank, played pool, darts, and pull tabs.

Every week I talked with Ricky a little more, learned more about him, and he stopped over here sometimes. I liked talking to him. He's hilarious."

"Did Ricky ever do his imitation of the Minions singing the National Anthem?"

"Yes, I thought I'd piss my pants. He is so damn funny, but he was nice, you know? He listened to me. I really came to like him and like him in a way I didn't expect."

Russ turned away from me. Not surprisingly, the next part pained him. "That night at the Lake Tavern I told Ricky how I felt, and I asked him if he liked me like that, you know?"

I nodded. I knew.

"We left together. I'd left my truck at the Hollister farm. Ricky said I should drive his car because he had a little more to drink than he thought safe for driving. We stopped at the approach. We were talking and then we were kissing."

I could only imagine how difficult it was for Russ to tell me these things or admit them to himself.

"When we left, the tavern had about emptied out. There were a few cars in the lot, but it was so late, I didn't expect anybody to be around. Those guys must have followed us. I looked up from kissing Ricky and all these guys were staring at us through the car windows. Creepy as hell."

Russ looked at me like there was something I could do to help him tell the story. "What happened next?"

"You don't know what it was like, Lorraine. They were laughing and yelling stuff. They pulled Ricky out of the car first. They grabbed me and I fought them, but they pulled me from the car too."

"Sounds like you were pretty outnumbered."

"Yeah, that's what I'm saying." Russ swallowed hard.

His eyes were pleading with me, but I didn't rescue him. "Then what happened?"

His breath was shallow and quick like he was picturing it in his mind and searching for a way to explain something about himself.

"I—I should have fought harder. Hell, I was bigger than most of them. The college guys were strong." Russ rubbed his face with his hands and paced. "Ricky fought." Russ blinked away tears, shook his head, and breathed out a small laugh. "That little crazy man, he threw back insults and punched at them. I just...I just said I wasn't a faggot." He cried and wiped at his nose and eyes with the back of his hand. "I climbed over the fence and ran as fast as I could across the field to the Hollister farm to get my truck."

Maybe a better person would have soothed Russ. I wasn't a better person. I was a person who found my friend beaten and alone and strapped to a fence. I stared at Russ and willed him to say the rest of his piece.

"I got my truck and drove home. I didn't stay and fight. I didn't go back for Ricky. I didn't call the sheriff. I went home and picked a fight with Kenny and went to bed."

"You let Kenny give you a beating."

"Yeah, I deserved it."

"Nobody deserves a beating."

There it was. There was the story. Russ told Ricky he liked him, made out with him, and then ran away when the scared haters came. He'd been hiding, not even going to see Ricky or telling the sheriff who did it. Hiding to protect himself. Part of me wanted to leave him standing there to think about what he'd done. Not like he hadn't been doing that already. Maybe I should just write down his mistakes in a notebook like my momma's registry of sin. But I wasn't my momma and I'd made a promise to Ricky, so I told Russ, "Ricky wants to see you. He's worried about you and he misses you."

"How could he, Lorraine? I ran away." Russ cried more as he stared into his big, callused, grease-stained hands. "I didn't know they would beat him."

"Well, you might have to tell yourself that for a while, but it was a crappy Judas-type thing you did." *Shit I sound like Momma or Grind throwing out Bible references.* "I doubt you thought they were there to throw Ricky a coming out party."

He glared at me a couple of beats. He took a deep breath, his fists were clenched, but he couldn't sustain the lie. "You're right, I knew they'd hurt him. Part of me thought he deserved it, that I deserved it too. I just ran. I'm a coward."

"A person, gay or straight, can't be expected to be brave every day. Maybe all we can ask for is the courage to be brave more often than we are cowards. Maybe that's all we can hope for."

"What am I going to do, Lorraine?"

"I don't know what you're going to do. The college guys got away with pulling you and Ricky out of the car and insulting you. Ricky was shot up with ketamine. He doesn't remember who beat him. I suspected there were two men from town who were behind beating him. One of the men came after Ricky and I was forced to shoot him. I think there's another man who got away with provoking the whole thing, but I can't prove it. He's probably not careless enough to come after Ricky again." I kicked around in the dirt. "As far as what to do now, I guess you've got to ask yourself what you want. Do you have feelings for Ricky? Are you prepared for the shit storm in your life if you declare you're gay?"

"Why is it still so hard? Gay marriage passed. I know people voted against it out here, but it's a law."

"Don't expect legalized marriage to stop some people from being afraid or hating. Laws change faster than hearts. If you don't believe me, ask a person of color if racism still exists in America. Tolerance is helpful, laws are necessary, but it's not the same as being truly accepted by somebody."

Russ turned and walked toward the house.

"Where're you going, what're you going to do?" I yelled after him.

Chapter Twenty-Seven

I WENT HOME to the farm. The sheriff's cruiser, an ambulance, and Twitch's Jeep were still in the yard. Dad waved me over to where he talked with Sheriff Scrogrum.

Ambulance attendants wheeled a gurney with a man bandaged and receiving fluids through his left arm.

"He's alive. Doctor Jacks?" I said.

"Yep." Dad removed his hat and wiped the inside with his bandana. "Did your momma tell you? How'd you figure it out?"

"Momma tipped me off when she reacted to me saying Ricky had been shot up with ketamine. Then I remembered what she'd said about all his vehicles, nice suits, and drinking at the Lake Tavern. It was a process of elimination after I'd already guessed wrong twice."

"It looks to law enforcement that Doctor Jacks went after Ricky. He got your momma to come to the clinic with a bogus report of a big emergency." Dad put an arm around my shoulder. He wasn't one to lower himself to gallows humor, but he said, "I bet he wishes he didn't wear such a nice suit out to our farm."

I snorted a slight laugh, but I felt sick that I'd shot a person. And I was relieved he wouldn't be coming after Ricky or me in our house again, although the image was already tattooed to my brain along with Becky.

"He's probably the jerk who called in the false report of a fire at the lumber yard. The voluntary firemen had to go over every inch of the place before we got the all clear." Dad coughed a bit. "I bet he was trying to keep Kenny and me in town while he had your momma wasting her time waiting at the clinic. All those lies gave him the chance to go after Ricky."

Dad said I should explain everything to Sheriff Scrogrum so that he didn't have to wait for Mumble and Shuffle to solve the crime. "Sheriff Scrogrum could use some success. Mumble and Shuffle are in the house taking pictures, shoving things in evidence bags, and measuring this and that throughout the house. Once they give the all clear, Twitch will start cleaning. Oh, and they're going to want your clothes."

"Budget cuts?"

"Funny, Lorraine." Dad called Sheriff Scrogrum over to where we stood. "Lorraine's here now. She can explain whatever I don't know or left out."

"I think I understand some of it myself. Let me get this straight." Sheriff Scrogrum scratched his head and jotted notes in a pad. "There were two cowhands taking the wires off Ricky's jaw when I got home today. They were supposed to be helping me find the guys who beat Ricky, but they were just trying to find out for Warren McGerber what Ricky remembered. I can't prove they worked for Warren McGerber, but it's true."

"I'll need to interview the cowhands." The sheriff marked some things in his long, skinny notebook.

"You can't interview them. I ran them off with a shotgun and one of them doesn't want to get caught for having sex with a minor."

"Right. So, this guy who's leaving in the ambulance, did he come with the cowhands?"

"No. I think the cowhands called Warren McGerber— I can't prove it. He got there late."

"Grind heard from Lewis and Petey about some college kids who were saying some hateful stuff that night at the tavern. Grind worried they had something to do with Ricky being hurt, so he decided to open the church as sanctuary for Ricky and for me if they could find me."

"Right, I thought Grind's the president of that group."

"He was, but he doesn't go for violence. He wants to stomp out evil, but he didn't want people literally stomping one another, especially when Grind realized that stomping might include his own daughter."

"They hurt the Grind girl too?"

"No, Charity is out of town and she's going to Europe. She's with someone else. Our relationship is over."

Dad touched my shoulder. "Aw Lorraine, I'm sorry. You've been through so much, kiddo."

"Thanks, Dad. Sorry, Sheriff, you don't need to know all of that. I'll stick to what happened with Ricky. When Pastor Grind realized that whoever hurt Ricky also learned Ricky would be able to talk tomorrow, he and McGerber opened the church and invited Momma to bring Ricky there to be safe and get his wires off a day early."

"So, who hurt Ricky?" Sheriff asked.

"Warren McGerber did, but I can't prove it. Doctor Jacks did and he's in the ambulance. The college boys pulled Ricky out of the car because some guys—probably Lewis or McGerber or Jacks—got them riled up thinking they were saving America from queers."

"I thought McGerber helped to keep Ricky safe?"

"That was J.C. McGerber," I said. "It was Warren McGerber, J.C.'s brother, who beat Ricky and tied him to the fence, but I can't prove it. It will all get blamed on Doctor Jacks. Warren McGerber calls it an act of God.

Warren is a good actor. He's trying to perform himself into congress."

"Right, so it was Warren McGerber's cigarette butts at the crime scene?" *Maybe they'll get him.*

"Probably, although I think Doctor Jacks takes a puff now and again too," Dad chimed in.

"Why'd he go across the field to the Hollister place?" the sheriff asked. "I suppose it's his boot print we found?"

That boot print belongs to Russ, but it's not mine to say.

"Is there anything left for me to do?" the sheriff said.

"Well, I suppose you need to put a warrant out on Lewis and Petey for their assault on Ricky at our farm and maybe they'll snitch on the others."

"Yep, that's already done." The sheriff looked thoroughly confused.

"Do I have to go to jail because I shot Dr. Jacks? I swear it was self-defense."

The sheriff slapped his notebook shut. "I know where to find you if the physical evidence and Mumble and Shuffle's inquiry prove you had culpability in this whole mess. I left an evidence bag with your dad. We'll need the clothes and shoes you were wearing."

Sheriff Scrogrum walked slowly to his cruiser.

"We better write this all out for the sheriff and drop the note off later," Dad said.

I agreed.

Chapter Twenty-Eight

MUMBLE AND SHUFFLE made quick work of the crime scene, which had once just been our farmhouse. They left only a few minutes after the sheriff. Immediately, Dad, Twitch, and I commenced cleaning. Our intentions were solid but seeing the living room in proper lighting showed the futility of our first idea. Ceiling plaster mixed with blood and water on the hardwood floor creating a sticky mauve paste that had to be mopped and scrubbed. Without speaking, Dad opened the side door of the house and he and Twitch dragged Ricky's blood-sodden makeshift couch bed outside. They let it roll down the hill on its metal castors until it crashed into the side of the burn barrel. While Dad retrieved some gasoline from the fuel barrel and then doused the couch I gathered up the blood-stained throw rug, the curtains, and the quilt Grandma had made.

Dad handed a box of wooden matches to me. "Would you like to do the honors?"

I struck a match and threw it onto the pile Dad had made soggy with gasoline. *Whoosh!* The curtains flared up for only a few seconds and were gone. The rugs burned more slowly giving off blue smoke and an acrid, chemical smell. Grandma's quilt seemed to dissolve. It wasn't long before the couch caught fire too and was reduced to a charred mass indistinguishable from what it had been. Dad tended the fire and soaked the ground around it with water from the garden hose. He wasn't about to let the fires of hell spread to anything unintended.

"Hold off on letting the dogs out of the barn," Dad said. "I don't want them getting into that blood. If you watch the fire, Twitch and I will take some Lysol to the walls and floors before we let them in the house."

Twitch poked his head out of the door and called to me. "I fixed the wires on the landline and there's a signal. I'm afraid I had to sweep up your cell phone and throw it in the bin. There was no resurrecting it."

I nodded. The smoke billowed away from me, so I took deep breaths and tried to send those memories and the stress of the day out of my body. By the time Dad joined me again the couch had burned down to its skeleton. I had no feeling for it. *It's just a couch. It has never been alive or part of my heart like Becky.*

"I sent Twitch home." Dad took the garden hose and extinguished the fire. He drenched the surrounding ground again for good measure. "Your momma called and said they're all still at Big Will's Diner and about to order pie."

"Still? It's been hours. Are you going?"

"I never say no to pie," he said. "You coming?"

"I will, but I'll drive myself."

"Don't take too long. She said Ricky's parents are there and his dad wants to meet you."

I smiled at Dad. He winked back at me. He got in his truck and drove toward the diner.

I opened the barn door. Pants, Sniff, and Satan went berserk jumping on me and racing to smell things. They circled the remnants of the fire and then raced to the house. I opened the door for them and they canvased the crime scene probably still detecting things Mumble and Shuffle had missed, and Dad and Twitch's cleaning couldn't eradicate. Dad had replaced the light bulb in the kitchen. When the dogs had enough sniffing, they settled at my feet while I sat at the kitchen table. I petted them a while and told them what had happened. They looked at me pensively—especially Satan. "It's going to be okay." To prove it I filled their bowls up with dog food and topped it off with Momma's famous meatloaf leftover from supper earlier in the week. Then, I drove to the diner.

MOMMA HAD COMMANDEERED the biggest table Big Will had and it appeared she planned to use the place until Big Will kicked her out. She sat with Dad on one side of her and Ricky's mom, Maria, on the other side. The blond-haired man next to Maria had to be Ricky's dad. Ricky sat next to him. Ricky's dad had his hand on Ricky's back between his shoulder blades. To my surprise Russ was seated next to Ricky. Kenny sat between Allan and Ramona. Allan's laugh rose in the air like the high notes on a piano as he played a game with Ramona.

I watched for a while and saw what had Allan giggling. Ramona took Allan's face in her hands and pretended she was about to kiss his messy, rosebud lips, but as she just about got to his lips she veered off in another direction and kissed his nose or eye or ear. You'd think Ramona's misdirection was the funniest thing Allan had ever seen and maybe it was. Then Allan did the same thing to Kenny. More giggles.

There was an open chair by Dad. I'm sure it was meant for me, but I couldn't take it. I was on the outside looking in, but it was okay. *I'm okay. Well, I'm good enough.* Without them seeing me I left the diner and drove back to the farm.

The papers from the college and the student loan application were anchored to the table by the hen and rooster salt and pepper shakers. I started with the college paperwork. They had demanded a final answer about when I would enroll. I warned them I would be there next semester. I wrote a check that emptied my bank account. I stuck it in the envelope, sealed and stamped it before I had a chance to reconsider.

Next, I completed the student loan papers. I was old enough to sign them myself and I was willing to incur some debt to finally finish my degree and practice as a vet for real. I stuffed those forms in an envelope, sealed and stamped it. I slapped the envelopes against the table as I contemplated the next more dangerous task.

Charity answered after a couple of rings but sounded irritable. "Lorraine, I said I'd call you when I knew what I wanted to do. I need more time."

"It's okay, Charity. You don't have to agonize over any decision. I'm half of this equation and I made my own decisions. I love you and would love to keep loving you, but I don't want to hang on to that while you're across the ocean. Of course, you should take this opportunity and I don't even care that you have it with Kelly—okay, that's a lie, but the point is I get it." I paced in the kitchen as I spoke. The dogs watched me like they were taking in a slow tennis match. The phone cord of Momma's harvest gold wall phone twisted in knots. "You want to be an artist and you'll risk whatever to make the best art you can. I've felt the same way about taking care of Little Man this past year. Little Man, I mean Allan is going to be okay. Momma and Dad are here, and Kenny met a really nice woman who seems to be good for him. And Allan. I can leave him now."

Charity was silent on the other end of the line.

"Are you there?"

"Yeah."

"I'm leaving for school next semester. I want to be the best, most well-trained vet I can be."

"Lorraine, are you breaking up with me?"

Did she laugh? "Yeah, I guess I am."

"I didn't see that coming."

Tell me about it. "Neither did I actually. Maybe since Ricky is finally safe and Allan has two parents, I can think more clearly about my own life and future."

"Wait, what happened with Ricky? Did they figure out who beat him? I hope they tore their heads off."

I didn't tell her I'd nearly accomplished just that with Dad's shotgun. "Yeah, it's been sorted as best as it can be for now. You need to ask your dad about it. He's quite a hero in the whole thing. I think you'd be proud of how he provided sanctuary for Ricky."

I gave Charity time to take that in.

"Charity, I put in my paperwork for college. I start next semester. Maybe you can call or write me to tell me how your travels and artwork are going and I could tell you about school?"

She didn't say anything right away. I hoped the pause was because she wondered if she would miss me. I knew I'd miss her, and I knew I would get through it. I'd survived worse.

"Talk to you later?" Charity said.

"You bet." My heart didn't shatter.

I'd been carrying two identical business cards in my pocket but hadn't used the number. The crest for Jewitt County Social Services was nearly rubbed off and the sheen was totally gone from both cards, but I could read the number. I dialed.

Marin answered.

"Oh, I expected to get your voicemail," I said.

"Sorry to disappoint you, should I hang up?"

"No, don't hang up."

"I'm kidding, Lorraine. I'm glad you called. Sheriff Scrogrum called me and told me you were very courageous and instrumental in saving Ricky again. No surprise there. He's asked for help from Mumble and Shuffle to launch further investigation."

"I wish I could believe they'll make short work of it. I do want to talk to you sometime about what happened, but that isn't the reason I called." I needed to take a big breath and hope I sucked in courage along with that oxygen.

"Lorraine? Are you still there?"

"Yes, I am." I took another deep breath and let it out with everything I felt in my heart right then. "I wanted to tell you...I want someone to be sweet to me too. It may sound weird, but I don't know if that's you exactly. I just know I like the way I feel being with you. I like how you treat me. I like the way you help people. I'm ready for your sweetness and I'm also ready to get on with college and become a real vet. It means I'll be away."

Marin didn't say anything, but she didn't just hang up either.

I kept going. "I'm going away to college next semester. I'll come back. I'll come back a lot because I will have a hard time being away from Allan, but I'm going to finish what I set out to do instead of waiting on anybody else to be ready. There'll always be something that could use my time and energy. I want to keep doing my work." I took another big breath. "If you can live with that I'd sure like to see you again."

I waited.

I worried my long speech had put her off or to sleep.

"You, Lorraine Tyler, are really sweet on me."

I know I blushed from head to toe. She was so sure of herself and listened to every word I said. We made a plan to meet again the next evening at her place for an indoor picnic. No horses. She told me it would be casual, clothes were optional.

Acknowledgements

Thank you, Raevyn McCann and NineStar Press for publishing *Stray*. Thank you, editors: Elizabeth Coldwell, Sera, and Tonna for helping to make *Stray* the best book it could be, and Natasha Snow for a stunning cover. Thanks to Sharon Belcastro and Ella Maria Shupe from Belcastro Agency for championing my work and believing that my stories had a place in the world. Thank you to my readers and all those folks who took a chance on reading my work.

My thanks to my siblings and their splendid partners and children for making my life richer.

About the Author

Nancy Hedin, a Minnesota writer, has been a pastor and bartender (at the same time). She has been a stand-up comic and a mental health crisis worker (at the same time). She wants readers to know that every story she writes begins with her hearing voices.

In 2018 Nancy's debut novel, Bend, was named one of twenty-five books to read for Pride Month Barnes and Noble and was named Debut Novel of the Year by Golden Crown Literary Society and Foreword Indies Honorable Mention for GLBT Adult Novel of the Year.

Email: njhedin@yahoo.com

Facebook: www.facebook.com/nancy.hedin.3

Twitter: @njhedin1

Website: www.nancyhedin.com

Also Available from NineStar Press

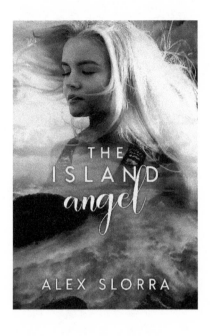

Connect with NineStar Press

www.ninestarpress.com

www.facebook.com/ninestarpress

www.facebook.com/groups/NineStarNiche

www.twitter.com/ninestarpress

www.tumblr.com/blog/ninestarpress

CPSIA information can be obtained
at www.ICGtesting.com
Printed in the USA
FSHW011148150919
61976FS